YOU AIN'T MY DAD

You Ain't My Dad

ARNOLD SHURN

authorHOUSE

AuthorHouse™
1663 Liberty Drive
Bloomington, IN 47403
www.authorhouse.com
Phone: 1 (800) 839-8640

Published by AuthorHouse 01/18/2015

ISBN: 978-1-5049-5838-7 (sc)
ISBN: 978-1-5049-5837-0 (e)

Print information available on the last page.

Any people depicted in stock imagery provided by Thinkstock are models, and such images are being used for illustrative purposes only. Certain stock imagery © Thinkstock.

This book is printed on acid-free paper.

Because of the dynamic nature of the Internet, any web addresses or links contained in this book may have changed since publication and may no longer be valid. The views expressed in this work are solely those of the author and do not necessarily reflect the views of the publisher, and the publisher hereby disclaims any responsibility for them.

CONTENTS

Acknowledgements... vii
Introduction... ix

Chapter 1:   X Factor.. 1
Chapter 2:   How it all began?.. 30
Chapter 3:   Sex "ain't" Love & Love "ain't" sex.................. 37
Chapter 4:   Who Really Benefits?....................................... 67
Chapter 5:   Raising a Child... 83
Chapter 6:   Frustration!.. 92
Chapter 7:   Mental State 106
Chapter 8:   Robbed of Fatherhood 112
Chapter 9:   Silent Tears 115

Acknowledgements

I want to start by thanking God for his grace and mercy. I would also like to thank God for bringing me out of the darkness and into a marvelous light of joy, peace, and hope. God I ask that the words I write be inspired by you. I dedicated this book to my mother Theresa Shurn who transitioned from this world on May 2, 2004, and to my dad Herbert Shurn who is my hero and an example of what a real man is. I also want to acknowledge my beautiful, lovely, daughter Terri who is my inspiration and motivation. I would also like to acknowledge my wonderful grandbaby that is a source of inspiration and for keeping me young at heart. I want to acknowledge my four brothers George, Ervin,(Skinny Brown) Corthaniel (Jim), and the babyboy Jerome (Romie Romie), who have transitioned from this world. I also want to give a shout out to my brothers in South Carolina who are not just talking the talk, but walking the walk. They are making a difference in our youth lives with their mentoring program ELITE (Empowering Leaders Innovators through Education). These men are examples of <u>MIGHTY </u>men of God. I want to thank anyone who has ever offered me a kind word, and those who have provided me time in their lives to vent and to cry on their shoulders. Thank you for the encouragement when I was discouraged and felt like this journey called life was too much to bear. I like to thank my immature and mature self for my life experiences that are shaping and molding me into the man I am evolving into today.

Last but certainly not least, I would like to thank my son who is the nucleus of my inspiration for writing this book. My experiences and opportunity to be a father was forfeited and all access denied. Despite the physical detachment, I still seek to have a personal, emotional, and human connection with my son. However, the opportunities are fading fast to do that.

INTRODUCTION

The book_You "Ain't" My Dad was inspired by a father's loss of his place in his child's life and the pain he suffered due to circumstances beyond his control. The pain became so unbearable it took its toll on his mental capacity to move forward. However, when he matured and understood that some things can't be controlled, He eventually overcame the pain. Those obstacles would not only impact his life, it impacted an innocent child's life. This child had no choice of who his parents were. The book explores the morals and spiritual decline of the family dynamic, and attempts to find answers to these obstacles. Through all those obstacles, he would discover that **God** had a greater purpose for him other than self –pity & self-destruction. This awakening allowed the renewing of God's purpose. This fatherless father is me, and I began to speak to the voiceless, to bring attention to the ills of social injustices that disenfranchised and separated fathers from their families. I no longer could carry this pain alone. The pain and the psychological scars I carried, as a fatherless father. I wanted to share my fatherless father experiences years ago, but I was powerless over the mighty hands of the legal system. I was defenseless over the powers to be, and I too fail victim to a hostile legal system that I was trying to avoid. This deceptive system made me another statistic- as another absent father. Despite all the anguish, I'm still trying to change the narrative about the perception of fathers. I am trying to right the wrongs of an unjust legal system that's determined to eliminate fathers from their natural position as the patriarch. This book is an effort to tell the story of a father who was denied an opportunity to be a father, and his efforts to gain his dignity. The world needs to know my side of the truth, which is I never abandoned my son! As a father, all I ever wanted was to be a father to my child and/or at least given an opportunity to do so. Is this an unreasonable request for a man to want to be present in his son's life?

I simply wanted to be a father, and play a role in my son's life. The child support system saw my role differently. They saw me as profit for their corporate investors! These private prison corporations are why fathers are being erased from their families and placed in prisons. The powerful system of injustice have made being poor a crime in this country, because legally it is still evident in the African American community. My community! From the eyes of an African American male, there are specific reasons why so many families are being raised by single mothers. These problems cannot be resolved instantly; however, by bringing a different perspective to this problem, individuals and a "willing" society can examine this crisis in its totality and have a constructive dialogue of what to do. This bias system uses men in jail to perform slave labor for major corporations. This constitutional amendment that allows this has to be changed first, so the system can be changed.

(Amendment XIII)
Section 1.

- Neither slavery nor involuntary servitude, except as a punishment for a crime whereof the party shall have been duly convicted, shall exist within the United States, or any place subject to their jurisdiction
- Congress shall have power to enforce this article by appropriate legislation.

The laws (**Legal Advancement White Society**) are detrimental to poor families. Unfortunately, as the problem stands, there are no solutions only finger pointing. They're profiting off of this fashionable term, "Dead beat dads." There are external and internal factors that have allowed this to become a crisis for families; in particular African American families. One major factor would be the legal system that produces an enormous amount of wealth off the backs of the poor. Maybe this book will be a source of inspiration for fathers who are victims of a flawed legal system. I'm going to pull the curtains open and reveal to the world the deception that goes on behind the curtain. The number of men who are denied their human rights to be fathers are alarming! These manufactured X factors are specifically designed to deconstruct and obstruct the family dynamics. Men's roles have been minimized to watching from inside a jail cell as spectators, or watching from the inside out in another mental state. This crisis of fatherless' homes is not something that suddenly showed up on our doorsteps. This was designed with a specific purpose in mind, which is to silence the voices of fatherless fathers and to eliminate their impact in "their children's lives." This book is not another 500 page exploration of all the woes and ills of our society from my point of view. This book will offer a glimpse of some of the scenarios in my life, and explore the options and offer my suggestions. There has been a plethora of recycled information written to address the social problems of the poor, and why it is important for fathers to be in the home. Why are fathers vanishing from the homes? I want to inform fathers who have been affected by these unscrupulous laws. The disappearing of the male from the family parallels to the drug epidemic experience in America. The drug war incarcerated and separated so many men from their families. It was not until white America began to feel the impact that it became a crisis in America, so the powers that be pronounced a war on drugs. They switched the war on drugs and are now concentrating on the war on black families! And like the war on drugs, it is a war on black men to increase the privately owned prison population.

Maturity has allowed me to understand that the choices I made, dictated my life and as a man I have to face the consequences of those choices. I will be the first to admit that I made unwise choices in life. I didn't foresee it would be a life sentence that I would have to bear. This book allows the reader to experience this journey through my lenses. I never would have imagined in a million years that I would still be waiting and staring out of the window hoping for my son's shadow to appear. My pain of guilt, sorrow, and hopelessness has never relinquished. My son who I love immensely will never see my cries and sleepless nights. He will never know the devastation of why dad was not there. With every breath I take, I am reminded of the choices I made or didn't make. There's this lurking question that lingers in my head. Have I exhausted every possible avenue to be a father? This question haunts me and tries to convince me that I could have done more. I have my moments of "would of, could of, and should of" symptoms that are a challenge to withdraw from. I am constantly trying to maintain my emotional sanity in a world that labels me a deadbeat dad.

I am a dead broke dad! I had been broken by a system that disguises their real intentions, which is to dismantle families. Their honest concerns are not for the welfare of the family. Their real agenda is to control, and to increase their Prison Industry Complex investment. I am not talking just to hear myself, here's my suggestion. I want the readers to do some research and follow the money trail of the supporters who are involved in building these private prisons. Do you think it's just by coincidence that schools in economically depressed communities around this nation are being torn down? Think about that one for a minute before you answer.

I want to express how my love and forgiveness was able to extinguish hate. Hate can destroy life's purpose! Hate denies the soul of a man to know peace and joy, of having the warmth of a loving hug, a tender kiss, or a passionate, purposeful conversation. I know about holding on to hate, because hate almost killed me! I had to forgive myself and others, so that I could live, and then to be forgiven by God first, and then by others. The travesty of love is that most people will never experience it in its true form, which is what I wanted to desperately give to my son. I wanted him to experience his dad's unconditional love. Maybe someone who reads this book can bring my dream into the future, and help make my dream a reality. My son and I deserve to be reunited. This book is my desperate plea for help. I am an old man now, and I have exhausted all avenues. I am going to believe in the familiar saying, "When prayers go up, blessing come down!" I just have to believe that there is a blessing coming out of this anguish and turmoil. For the men who are experiencing this legal kidnapping of their children, **I say don't lose hope!"** God's going to turn it around and help us reunite with our precious children. My suggestion to the fatherless father is to hang in there, and don't ever give up hope of reuniting with your children. Never stop believing! Hope and Faith is all that's left. I hope this book can build bridges, and help tear down these walls of division among our families.

CHAPTER 1

X Factor

Mothers that have the job of parenting have a life time job, as many of you already know; this should include the fathers too. It saddens me that I was not provided an opportunity to fulfill my lifetime position as a father, because of internal and mostly external factors beyond my control. Yes, I am in total agreement that the non-custodial parent should fulfill their share of the financial responsibility. No father should ever be exempt, or be allowed to take a financial vacation; therefore, there will be absolutely no opposition on my behalf. My opposition comes in the form of how the process is currently being executed. It is the child support agency's hostility and the criminalization of the fathers that is my concern, and this is what I'm fighting to improve. I am not angry that, I had to pay child support. I am angry because I was **NOT** allowed to see my son, so yes I am resentful against the **Child Support Enforcement Agency** for that reason. Yes, I resent them for locking me in jail and taking my driver's license at a drop of a dime. Who in their right state of mind wants to go to jail, and who mandates a man to go to jail for having a baby? Then to add insult to injury, I was denied visitation rights base on a judge's personal feelings. There is something fishy going on here.

During the time this book was being written there has been some slight changes made in the hostile and criminalizing of fathers; however, it is not enough to mention so I "won't". There have been some band aids put on bullet wounds type solutions. For example, the **Fatherhood Initiative Programs** are not of optimum benefit to the father without support of the community and massive funding from the government, or from those that support the fathers inclusion in the family. As things stand now, nothing is being offered to prevent my brothers from becoming another number in prison. These programs look good on the surface, but do nothing to address or provide the needs of the fathers who are victims of an unfavorable "just us" system. They are reactive programs that appeal to the public perception that the problems of single mothers is being addressed. The solutions for these fathers are economic empowerment, affordable housing and homeownership, spiritual healing and mental counseling. These fathers need the same opportunities afforded to the single mom to impede oppression spurred on by poverty and social injustice. This leads to the detachment of fatherhood and manhood. Without a roadmap to empowerment and resources, fathers are reduced to an animalistic state of survival (Survival of the fitness). **Suggestion Moment: When a man has a job, and he can contribute to his family, his manhood is restored. Basically, I am saying a livable wage job can restore hope and change the dynamics of the family structure. Poverty and jail is the opposite result of hope and prosperity. To have a real impact in these impoverished communities and this may be wishful thinking; there needs to be the same financial enthusiasm to combat poverty and create job opportunities that there is to build prisons.**

History has proven that justice is not always swift, it moves all too often at a tortoise-like speed for the disenfranchised minorities who have been dehumanized, marginalized, and categorized as less than human beings. This sector of our population does not have the financial ability to influence and balance the scales of an unjust system. They unfortunately are the ones who will often see the color blind injustice. The system has never been inclusive for all Americans to obtain upward mobility. I'm not talking about black people only. I'm including the working class who are ignorant of the facts that they are getting tricked too by their "poli "trick" ions."

Light and darkness cannot co-exist. Why? Because light will always illuminate darkness and the light is the truth. The eyes can only see when they are open to see the truth. Some people will always accept the darkness of a lie and shut out the light of truth, and avoid the truth as if it doesn't exist. It's like what the Gospel group the Winans said; "What is the world coming to?" It seems like everyone is running from the truth." The truth takes people out of their comfort zone, and makes them take a look at themselves. This is something some Americans refuse to do. Nevertheless, while searching my inner soul, I found that there were some things I didn't like about myself, and if I wanted to become a better man I had to change. I believe this should apply to America as a whole. If America wants to truly live up to its creed of life, liberty, and the pursuit of happiness, and that all men are created equal then the same can be said of us, we all need to change. There's a saying in the rooms of the fellowship that says, "It is important to get brutally honest in order to make a real change." **Well, if the truth is the light, shine some light on the truth as to why the fathers are not present in the home?**

This brutally honest thing led to unlocking some of the mysteries of **SELF,** which was **not an easy venture**. I was in denial about some things about myself, and I was still holding on to the old me. I quickly learned how to cover up the defects of my character, and act like they didn't exist. Therefore, I could avoid facing the truth, and I could continue to wear the mask. I could continue to blame others for my irresponsibility. It's like that elephant in the middle of the room; I would avoid it or go around it. But just because I ignored it, didn't mean the elephant wasn't in the room. It was time to clean up my house, and sweeping everything under the rug was no longer sufficient. After a while, that trash starts to stink. Eventually, this trash had to be removed from under that rug, because the odor became unbearable even for me. The problem I faced was how long was I willing to allow my life to stink? I had to take the trash out and keep it out, and for me to do that I had to clean places that I didn't know were dirty or even existed.

The problem is that many of these manufactured "X factors" are purposely designed to cause havoc in the family structure. These X factors are manufactured to alienate the father and to create indecisiveness; therefore, excluding any possibilities of an amicable solution. This creates what I call the tug of war affect. The families ignore these X factors by attacking each other or completely denying that they even exist. By constantly accepting the ploys of the X factors, it becomes normal **not** to have a father in the home. The time has arrived where a thorough examination is needed to understand this phenomenon. As to why fathers are in this condition; and what can society do to change it? If families continue to accept that there're no major underlying issues, our families will remain in disarray and will be obliterated. Parents we have got to change the perception of non-custodial parents, so that a functioning relationship can be established for both parents. Ladies can start by, stop telling your baby's fathers that you don't need him, and telling that innocent child that his father "ain't" shit! It serves no purpose other than to destroy the family. This only creates an angry and vindictive child. What will that child do with this anger as he/she evolves into adulthood?

Mothers, stop falling for this set-up game, because these manufactured X factors are getting two for one. The set up game is like playing the shell game. The shell game keeps you guessing where the ball really is. The system is the same way. It will have you to believe that they are for the advancement of the family by offering you more than one of the X factors. In actuality, they are **NOT** for the family at all. They are there for their personal gain. It's all deception, so where is the ball?! Just when you go to pick the ball in the middle, you find out, it's not really there. The slightest movement of hands will have you deceived and confused. Now, how does the X factor affect my baby's daddy? Why is my baby having trouble in school? Through the deception they have the daddy in jail for his financial disability, and you have an angry child who they calculate and expect to fall victim to their systematic plot. It's deception. Ladies. Remember ladies everything isn't always what it appears. The child will probably become defiant towards their mother. They will prescribe him medication, but mom ignorantly allows it because now the child is docile and she can control him. Mom will not mind, because now the boy is docile and she can control him. The downfall is he becomes less expressive. There is a term in the Diagnostic and Statistical Manual; Fourth Edition (DSM- IV-TR) called *Oppositional Defiant*. Yes, I know, they have a diagnosis for everything now! The reason they have so many diagnoses is so they can make money! It's called billing. Back in the day, the old folks use to say, "That boy has a lot of energy, or let that boy go outside and play. Give him something to do." Now it's, "Give that boy his meds so he can sit down and be quiet!" Parents, when you give your child meds, you have just helped the system kill your child's mind; therefore, killing his creativity and his ambitions.

Check out this scenario: In school your poor baby is being documented (labeled) as a defiant child, because he is vociferous in his expression. He is suspended for his actions because his 23 year old, white, female, teacher only knows about black boys, and girls of color through her one credit hour cultural sensitivity training course. Her experiences come from watching negative portrayals of black boys on the "Tell -a Lie- Vision" (television) to form her views. She has no prior interaction with young African American males until her first day in the classroom, so she fears that black boy who tries to express himself from her preconceived images. She writes him up, so documentation can now follow the child, and suspension becomes a normal activity to alleviate her fears. (Go do your research, and tell me what you discover about the suspension rate of African American boys.) She wants to make her classroom conducive to learning, and disruptive outbursts are not allowed. They have taught her that you must always be in control and manage any classroom. Putting them out becomes her management control. If it was me, I would have taken this child's enthusiasm, and turned it into a fun, learning sitituation. I would have had him write his own rap song or a poem. I would create venues in which he could express himself freely. I would have found a creative way to channel that energy into something productive. That's just my ideal, having worked in that environment many times. In the defense of the school teachers, (because I don't want to throw them under the bus) there are some situations where there is no other alternative but to document the child's behavior, if the child has in fact been diagnosed **properly** with Attention Deficit Hyperactivity Disorder (ADHD) or Attention Deficit Disorder (ADD).

The plan of the X factors is for this child to become a member of the Prison Fraternity Complex Industry. If that plan is not successful, he falls into the hands of the pharmaceutical industry. Either choice is not a good one! Eventually, he does become defiant because now school is not the place where he can express himself. To him it is a hostile environment. He either has to conform or get suspended. If he can't express himself in school, where can he express himself? Home, no he can't do it there either. At home he has all kinds of gadgets (X-boxes, cell phones, and social media) that limit his expression and creativity. The single mother is too fatigued to listen, after coming home from working two jobs and going to school full time. I know the question is lurking, so I'll ask it for you. **Where is the father?** He's probably caught up with his own self pity, pain, hopelessness, depression, financial instabilities, and addictions. To answer the question, I don't know. Ask the mother if she knows.

This is the cunning tactic that is used to get the two for one deal. Mom you've allowed a third party to control the parenting in your house, and when you let those folk downtown in your business, it ends up being a bad option for our families. I would advise you to **NEVER** let them in! When you put them folk's downtown in your business, families becomes more divided and our situation becomes **catastrophic.** This is one of the many devices that they use to set the ignorant family up for the prison pipeline. They keep the family confused and divided. Black men and women have to learn to become each other's help-mates. The relationship with the mother of our children does not have to be about drama. Relationships that are loving and respectful can have positive results and benefits for the child.

If the truth be told, there has always been a systematic attack to minimize the African America fathers, since they were brought to the shores of America centuries ago. There were unspeakable things done to the male in front of the black female to instill fear. This fear still exists, for example, the killing of black boys by police officers. This put the black women into the position where she has to become the main protector of the entire family. She teaches the black male to be passive and not to buck the system for fear of his life. She's hoping this is enough to keep the male family member safe. This takes the black male out of his natural position to guide, instruct, and protect his family. This should be the natural order of things according to the King James Version of the Bible. His ability to pursue liberty, justice, and happiness has become compromised at the hands of others since his abduction. His psychological scars are too deep to heal, and his constant battle never ends. This holds true for the **strong** black women too, but she was allowed a **temporary** sense of **false hope**. This delusional hope would come in the form of separation of power, and false dominion over her male counterpart. She was led to believe that she did not need the male to provide for her. This continues to hinder the emotional balance of the family structure. The woman was made from the male's rib. God made her to be the "**HELP** MATE!" not "THE MATE." God said man is the head of the household. It's a good thing "When a Man finds a Wife! Not the other way around. Not only should he leave money for his children, but also his grandchildren. When a man can't feel like a man, his only option is to feel like a WOMAN! Now the roles have been reversed, therefore, having a reverse effect on the family. If women are forced to play the role of men, then men have no choice but to play the other role/gender, FEMALE (X factors again!). The man has now been forced into a role that was not given to him by God! Biblically speaking, neither two men, nor two women can make a spiritual, mental, emotional, healthy, stable family base (God made Adam & Eve, **NOT** Adam & Steve.) They have switched and reversed the roles of power between the black man and woman systematically. These meetings were held behind closed doors between the 1% of white men who actually control this system/country. Women were meant to be the other gun, and other eye, (that means BACK-UP.!) Not the other way around! Now In my eyes, the solution is education and job opportunity (It would also help if police officers didn't use black men as target practice.) If the system would reverse the roles to their proper positions, by giving black men job opportunities in higher positions, the black family would have a better chance of surviving successfully. My point is, that if the battle is shared, it would be easier for black men and black women to face their challenges together instead of apart! This would increase their chances of defeating these manufactured X factors that are keeping families divided and from having harmony. Black people are not operating in their natural rhythmic vibrations that have produced the fortitude to overcome centuries of adversities. Our problems have become departmentalized and individualized, and now the wool is being pulled over our eyes. The same methods were utilized to colonize Africans by their oppressor by giving a few blacks that false pride of authority. They would become naïve participants in their own enslavement. When they did become aware of the deceitfulness of the oppressor, the damage had been done. The oppressor was able to reign over the Negro, because of his power to deceive a few. The Negro never saw it coming, and the oppressors theory of divide & conquer is still prevalent today in the African American community. This impact is like small pox was to the Indians, or malaria is to Africa. It has killed them physically and spiritually. This **spiritual death** has had the greatest impact. This kind of death is one that is very difficult to recover from, because it attacks not only the essence of the soul, it robs one of their hopes and dreams. How does a person exist in a world without hopes and dreams? I find it difficult today, and the state of hopelessness is a dark place to be. When I felt like I had no purpose to exist, I sought and found my hope in a bottle of Mad Dog, commonly called MD20/20. **In my despair, false hope was better than no hope.**

Mentally we are fearful from detaching from our oppressors, so we attack those who are in our proximity. This hate has been passed down from generation to generation, and it is evident in the African American communities. It's like being agitated with your employer, but you can't take your anger out on him/her because your job is your life line. So what do you do? You go home and take it out on the kids or your wife. Hell, you might even kick the dog! The point here is when a person feels helpless and worthless they will transfer that frustration somewhere else. Because my people are confused, we will cause havoc on our own communities. In other words, the pain that is perpetuated upon us will be perpetuated upon another. The other just happens to live next door and look like you.

The saying goes, "A problem shared is a problem solved." It is unfortunate that some men have not grasped the pain and suffering, in which our strong black women have endured. After all that they have endured, it would seem that the black man would be eager to love and protect his black woman even more. The black women are women beyond ordinary women! **They gave birth to a nation!** Some black men have taken the essence of their womanhood and walked all over their loving and nurturing ways, and subjected black women to the same mental, emotional, physical, financial, and sexual abuse the slave master/owner subjected them to. What does that say about the black man? This is a clear indication that some black men are really sick and have not fully recovered from their mental psychosis. They are in need of emotional, spiritual, and mental healing. When I say "WE", I am talking about the black female and male, who are obviously dealing with some identity crisis issues and some self-worth issues. They have taken on the unnatural spirit of the European Caucasian (White People). God bring my people out of darkness, and out of the bondage of self-hate and self-annihilation. When I look into my brother's eyes, I can see that blank stare of death that comes from depths of despair. If the eyes are the windows to the soul; then somebody better get some Windex cleaner, so that the light of salvation can shine through that despair. My brothers I hear your cries. Please just hold on help is on the way, because the dead will rise again, but when, I don't know? I hope it's sooner than later because black folks have been waiting on a savior for a mighty long time. I wonder if it is possible to save ourselves, while waiting on our savior.

Black men are suffering from a mental psychosis and the psychological effects of slavery and economic deprivation, which I witness every day. Many of my brothers' are in a zombie like state of mind or in a vicious downward cycle of self- hate, which leads to abnormal behavior. I see some of my brothers hanging on the street corners or in front of the Palestinians stores trying to escape their hopelessness. Some of them have become so dissatisfied with their perception of reality; they will choose an alternative route. This route may seem easier at the time, but it comes back to bite them in the ass. One method that has not worked is trying to escape the hardship of their lives by using mind altering drugs. For those of us who are not avoiding reality we are in the churches praying for a God to save us from the evils of this corrupt world, because the world around us is crumbling. There you have it, you got brothers in the church praying for hope, and you got the other brothers cross the street from the church looking for hope through dope by putting a needle in his arm. The other brothers got a crack pipe in his mouth; then you got the brother hooked on pills and alcohol. There you have a group of brothers praying for a way out, and the other group of brothers dying for a way out. Just take look around or venture out into the urban war zones and into the homes of our people. You have boys and young men who think it is fashionable to stand on street corners exposing their posterior to the world. Many believe that this behavior initiated from men in jail as an indicator to other men in prison that they wanted another man to put dick up your ass. Our ancestors didn't die for this shit, come on people it is time for a reality check. This saggin, as it is called; began as a psychological ploy during slavery to disadvantage the slave from wanting to escape from the plantation. They would take the apparatus used to hold the pants of the slave up, so it would be difficult for a slave to run away from the plantation. If the slave did run away, it would impede the success of their escape; so they thought. This was another device used to humiliate, brain wash, and instill control over the minds of the slave. The young men on the street corner call this style saggin. **I wrote a poem about want hear it?**

Poem: **Pull Your Pants Up**

The cliché, "I wear the pants in this house, and I am not afraid of another man, because I put my pants on just like him." During that era it symbolized responsibility, authority, and courage. However, today the representation of how a man wears his pants has a different connotation. Now it is about this distorted representation of building a reputation, with this new generation.

I've begged them please, but they still wear their pants below their knees. They say, "Man this is sag." I tried to explain to them that style originated from prison, and it represented that you were a fag. I explain that you don't have to sag, but you can have swag (Standing With Absolute Greatness). Furthermore, I explained the historical context of saggin: saggin is niggas spelled backwards, and was a tactic for slave master to keep niggas dehumanized.

Nevertheless, they go on about their merry way, so I guess their saying it is cool to be that way. Well, why stop there, if you're going to wear your pants below your knees? You might as well put your butt up in the air, and wave it like just don't care because obviously you want another man to go there.

Real men don't sag, so pull your pants up on your waist, and stop this human disgrace. Young men show some class, and stop acting like you want another man to put some dick up your ass.

> *I know every generation had their fashion styles. I am trying to inform and give some context to the originality of that style. And allow them the freedom of choice to make an educated and informed decision.*
> *The Messenger Feb, 2010*

Check this out, take this word saggin and reverse the spelling; it spells "NIGGAS." What's the definition of a nigga? A nigga is an **ignorant** axx fool. Who do not know anything and refuse to want to know anything, or do anything, so he ends up being nothing but a nigga. Wake up! Wake up! My people are perishing from the lack of knowledge. I do not know where my people going to find some self-worth or where it will be found. It is time to pick up our shovels and start digging for hope somewhere. These children are looking for your attention, and they are crying out for our help. The black community is in such disarray they have no knowledge of the disconnection with our youth's. Where are the pillars of our communities? Where are warriors who have the valor and readiness to fight for freedom and Justices? Where are you? I know you are out there somewhere hiding. Calling on all men of morals and standards, it is our responsibility to tear down the false imagery of the media. We have to tear down these walls of deception and build our young men up with tough love. Men of morals and standards it is our job to dispel the deception that black men are not capable of loving and honoring their black beautiful women. Men of morals and standards it is our responsibility to display to our young men an alternative life style, other than the ones that are manufactured by those X factors.

One of these manufactured **X** factor is the Hollywood Industry, known for promoting negative images to persuade our children fragile minds. These imagines are making it acceptable to have sex, to kill, and to degrade women. Degrade our women to the point that is acceptable to treat them less than animals. Why have this become acceptable among a loving and passionate people who have always strive for excellence? I am asking real men to take off the mask of fear, and go out amongst them and transform their ignorant ways. This is a role call for men of morals and standards. It is time to lift every voice, and provide these ignorant teenagers and young men an alternative life style. Show them that they too can become men of morals and standards. Stop this hate and criminal activities towards one another, because it impedes the progress black people have made. Black people have fought too hard and too long for justice. The killing of our sisters and brothers makes no sense! **Wrote a poem about it want to hear?**

POEM: **Brothers**

Black on black crime- isn't it time for us to stop getting angry and losing our minds; just to kill our own kind? For some senseless, I don't know why I did crime. Brothers we got enough obstacles in our way

without having to worry if we are going to be killed by a so called brother today.

Brothers do you realize that we're walking and running the same race, and brothers it's not about what's yours or what's mine we must stop with this killing of our own kind. We must do away with this black on black crime; because brothers I don't have a dime and I got to work just to get mine.

And it's no longer the Jim Crow laws or us being lynched from a tree, death today comes by the way of a brother who looks just like me. Brothers are killing brothers every day we got to find a positive solution, because this "ain't" the way. We got to stop polluting our sister and brothers with all this dope, and give them a future and array of hope.

We got to stop this envy, disrespect and strife. Want we need to do is focus on living a more productive life. Brothers it is time for us to come to the table of brotherly love so we can show one another that it's going to take respect sharing and love to uplift one another, because after all you are all my brothers.

Now fast forward to the twenty first century, and you have a system predicated on propaganda, which labels a man a dead beat dad. This has nothing to do with the natural potential of the father to raise his child, but a systematic plan to distort the natural role of the father, and to create the public deception that your economic status is the only barometer that needs to be measured for the legitimacy of fatherhood. This creates a vacuum in the family, and leaves women to be the sole protectors and providers of the family. They are no longer using the brutal fear tactics they used in eighteen and nineteen century, but modern tactics of taking your economical freedom and your dignity. This creates the same conclusion that the past tactics resulted: division, separation, economic disenfranchisement amongst the community and family. Again, creating division between the male and female, and making the male appear weak and useless. The natural role of men and women are being tampered with in numerous ways, while some are apparent and others are not so apparent.

A man doesn't feel like a man when he cannot contribute to his family, and realistically that is all he wants to do. He wants to look the world in the face and hold his head up proudly as a man, and claim his share of dignity.

The black female was left with no options. She was **forced** to be dominant and stay strong; because that was the only way she could sustain her family and maintain some sort of dignity. She had to be strong for so long, and when her role was asked to be reversed to its natural order the mental damage and identity crisis was too deeply embedded to be reversed. It is frustrating that the media betrayal of the Black African Colored Negro American family is presented in a negative and inaccurate way. What they have done is fabricated the truth. The strong black women had to be strong to maintain and protect her family for centuries due to the construct of slavery. This theory that the male has always been in control of their household has not always been realistic. This is not factual for the Africans descendants enslaved here in America. The strong black males were **forced** out of their natural role, by the evilness of slavery. They were subjugated by different morals, spiritual, and mental brain washing for centuries. Their names were taken; language, spirituality, and the essence of their souls were taken. Who else have endured such continuous demonic atrocities? Yes, others were oppressed and enslaved, but nothing remotely compares to the evilness in which chattel slavery was force on God's original people. Nothing!

~ The point must come when black people believe that they are somebody. Nobody else can do this for them, and they must truly trust God. Being the first humans that God created they must take ownership of their anointed authority, and show the world the power of pure blackness. We got to reverse the negative narrative of our blackness, and embrace the beauty of self. The oppressor has tried to twist the truth, and embrace their whiteness as pure and good, and depict God's **black people** as dark and evil. They switch good and evil to control the world perception. Many of our great leaders of the past tried valorously to encourage the black nation to embrace their blackness, but the psychological damage of slavery was entrenched into their mental and spiritual life. They are trapped in trying to be accepted in a world that has never accepted them, and in my opinion never will. I say, black people (the original people) need to stop expending so much energy on people who have shown that they don't love you or care for you. They tolerant you and that's a difference. It's like being in a relationship, and there is only one person displaying love. This type of love is loveless. My friend describes it like this, "it is like waiting for a boat at an airport," it's never coming. Black people stop waiting, and go to the dock and get on the love boat.

Question: Why do Black people always have to defend being black, and when will they start elevating and speaking about black economics and empowerment? They are now viewed as radicals and against the America's White Supremacy system. They are out to take back the country and make white people their subjects. Nigga Please! Why when black people begin to talk about gaining resources and awakening their people they become a threat to humanity? The White power groups' churches are not bombed and they are not put into jail when they speak about maintaining their whiteness. While wearing their white sheets, blue uniforms, black robes, and pinstripe suits in the Whitehouse. Okay, I diverted. Let's get back to the self-hate.

A: I do not believe that white people want to face their defects of character, because if they acknowledge the wreckage of their past, that means taking accountability and responsibility for their action. On the other hand, black people have closed the door on their dark evil past, and do not want to revisit it. We have two group of people who are in denial of their past, so the past to them never happened. This has created this deep rooted combustible hate boiling inside of the oppressor and the oppressed. The oppressor hates the oppressed and the oppressed hate being oppressed, so they love their oppressor out of fear. It like the rape victim blaming herself for the way she dress, and not the fact the rapist raped her and robbed her of her self-dignity. It easy to blame the victim, that way the oppressor can rationalize his immoral act.

This has created hatred for self, and the love and respect for those who have enslaved blacks mentally. For example, take a visit into the hood, black folks will build up and support every business that occupy their neighborhood. People that don't look like them or care about them, can open up any type of business, and become a success story. Sadly, I ony this, they can open up a business selling shit, and black folks will be the first in line with money in both hands ready to spend their hard earn money on some shit. As long as they convince them the shit is good for them, or that it will make them more acceptable. They will gladly purchase whatever is being sold without question. **Have we become so culturally conditioned to believe that we cannot do for ourselves? Have Black African American Colored Negro's reached a place of no return psychologically?**

This reminds me when my partner and I open up our restaurant, and man everyone wanted a hook-up. They didn't even respect that we were trying to be legit business owners. They would walk right out of our restaurant and go next door and spend their money on the hormone injected chicken from the Palestinian's gas station. Man these were people we knew and were down with us, and though wanted to see their homeboys from the hood succeed. We had a nice place and quality food, and a soothing environment. We had large blown up black historical figures on the wall, a large fish tank and a pool table. In all fairness, I cannot blame it totally on my people. I don't think we planned for success because we had no parking space, so that may have been the culprit that did us in, and the fact we didn't have enough startup capital. Unlike the Jewish community we did not have the support services needed in our community to succeed. We didn't have the capital or the wisdom to maintain and grow a business. If help was there we didn't know how to access the information, and again that was our fault for the lack of planning and research. Okay, I say 80% was on us, and the other 20% was on my people for our failure. Okay, 99.9% was on us. Okay, I can't blame my people for this one.

This is where the mental illness comes into play, I call it **consumerism psychosis**. This is when a person takes his/her money and spends it on things that have no value, and does not use their wages to increase what they have earned. For example, you have these so called celebrity or famous people who earn a tremendous amount of money. I have no problem with people getting their paper, but what they spend it on is outrageous and ridiculous. They could spend a meager portion of those earnings building, and buying property in the decaying urban areas. They can build and create a foundation where they can get a tax deduction, and take care of their community and family without going bankrupt, by going the foundation route. They can create job opportunities for others, and that would have far more of an impact than how many points you've scored or a NFL / NBA championship. Individual wealth will not and has not sustained us as a people. They can build a real legacy outside of the sport and entertainment arenas. They can be the catalyst to build future generations.

I am reading a book by William C. Rhoden titled the *Forty Million Dollar Slaves,* he point out the difference and the sense of pride an athlete had as black people, and the disconnection that the ignorant black athletes have towards the plight of their people and community. He goes on to describe how black athletes have been eliminated from baseball, horse racing, bicycling; because they didn't control the commodity of the sport. These were sports black athletes once dominated. The same is happening now in sports and in our community. What good financially does it serve the African American community? How many jobs are created in the front offices, and what T-shirt and other licensing deals do the black entrepreneurs have because of their talented entertainers and sport figures? How many black businesses been generated because of million dollars stadiums and black athletes'? How many schools been built?

Another example, the working poor will buy luxurious clothes and cars, but are renting property or living in the basement of their grandmother's house. You have Ray Ray and Short Breeze in the hood boasting about what they paid for those twenty- fours. The dam rims cost more than the car itself. This is stupidity at its best; not understanding economics. Ignorant is ignorant whether you rich or poor. It does not matter if you have three hundred or three million dollars, if you don't know how to manage money, the end result is broke. This is where those warehouses (schools) are failing our children. The garbage that is put in our children in these prison prep schools has no benefits. Other than, to remain in poverty and corner the market on low paying jobs, and to work pay check to pay check. This path often leads to the modern day plantation (prison). In the words of the freedom marcher, "We shall overcome someday." I know, I may sound like a scratched 45 album, but we must find a way to do for self, and to create our own wealth. This will only come to fruition, if we learn to love ourselves. Man, I tell you this chasing of the America dream can get frustrating; when you working pay check to pay check.

I wrote a poem about it want to hear it?

Poem: Can I get paid?

I don't mean to make no fuss, but this job got my life all messed up
it's like I am still riding on the back of the bus. This job got my life in
an uproar, because I'm tired of being classified as the working poor.
If I'm going to go to work and still be poor;
Then what the heck am I working for.

It seems the more hours I work, the less I make.
And the more that they decide to take.
People when are we going to get our tax break?
I go to work every day and I still can't gain any wealth,
And beside they don't even want to pay for my health.

Brothers this job got my life in a wreck, because I'm just like all the
rest of the 46 million
Uninsured I'm living pay check to pay check.
I've been in the cheese lines, welfare lines, unemployment line, and
now they got me standing in the check cashing advance line.

Gas prices are sky high and I can barely getting by.
Maybe this is why my brothers and sisters turn to dope, because they
just don't see no hope. People it's time for us to come to the realization
that we are all in the same boat,
And we're hanging on by a very, very thin rope.

We're all trying to live that American dream by working that 9 to 5,
but we're barely staying alive and working that J O B, that keeps us
just over broke.

I got a job, but on pay day, it seems like I'm being strong armed
robbed.
Brothers this job got my life in a wreck; I'm tired of living pay check
to pay check.

And in the words of Fanny Lou Hammer I'm sick of tired of being sick and tired…. of being sick of being sick and tired of working pay check to pay check.

Oh well, let me go to work so I can get a pay check.

Suggestion moment: First of all when public education was created it was designed to train children for the supply and demands of that time. The public school systems that many of our children attend today are antiquated. The inner city schools are not preparing children for the new economic opportunities of today. What is the point I am trying to present? If one would take a third eye observation of the world outside of America, they would discover that America investment in the public school system is a joke compared to other industrialized countries. The solution is not always money, it's the purpose and the end result achieved from an education. The new booming industry is technology, and Asia, North and South Korea are making major human investment in those areas. Their children are learning coding, computer language, and are making games and creating apps on phones, before they get out of high school, and can speak a few languages. While here in America our children are being prepped for the growth prison industry. Does anyone remember when public schools actually taught children a skill ready education? The public school students after high school could immediately transition into the job market. But now there's a host of for profit schools, because worthless education has grown into an enormous business. These colleges should be held under investigation, and held liable for providing students with worthless degrees.

Here's the hope shot, in order for our children to have a chance at economic freedom (we) all concerned citizens must unite in this fight for equality. This is not about black and white; it's about doing what's right. Because not having the educational resources, has an effect on all our children. The systems have to reinvest in teaching our children math, science, java, foreign languages, and how to create and design applications. This must be done quickly, because this is the new industry that has replaced the depleted car and steel industry that our parent's relied on in the past to feed and support their families. Parents this is our new civil right battle to secure an education that will allow our children to be globally competitive. Yes, great strides have been made in the battles fought by African Americans, but they cannot rest on their laurels. The American working poor cannot continue to be deceived that the race has been won. There is too much work left to be done on the battle fields to secure equitable education. The victory lap cannot be run yet. There were people who died for our right to have rights. Freedom is not free and we must never forget, because once we forget history it will be reinvented, and our freedom will be lost to our lackadaisical effort to retain it.

Once upon a time education paid off, and it paved a path to economic freedom, but today parents you should reconsider putting your children in a pile of debt for a worthless Liberal Art degree, and a job that pays a meager 15, 000 dollars a year. In my pursuit of the American dream, I am now in 130,000 dollars worth of debt and growing, which will take me two or three life times to pay off at my current salary. The sad part about this is that I have not died the first death yet. Maybe I should give this debt to my cat, because he has a better chance of paying off this debt than I do. My cat has nine lives, and I only have one. Parents this is something to seriously think about. Why are we sending our children to school every day; for what? If they are going to obtain a higher education the benefits must out weight the cost. Why pay all that money just to get a job? **I wrote a poem about want to hear?**

College Degree

I'm no longer living life happy, joyous, and free since I earned this worthless college degree. I was stress free before I earned my college degree. I thought I was going be financially set, but all I inherited was a degree and this enormous debt. My heart aches when I hear the phone ring, and today I look back with regret. I still have not achieved this financial security yet!

I dreamt of getting my degree, so I could pull myself up by the boot straps, and live out that American dream, but instead I'm so broke I'm living like a dope fiend. I got a job, a college degree and still can't

get these handcuffs off of me. I feel like I'm still in jail without a bail, and all I wanted was to live the American fairytale. Instead, I'm living a life of hell.

Now they want all this money back from me, but how am I going to pay it with this worthless college degree? I don't feel like I'm ever going to be happy joyous and free with all this pile of debt from this worthless college degree.

We will buy stuff to make us feel good on the outside, which does nothing for our families' future. We reside in the hood (that's what they are calling it now); it was once called a neighborhood. There is a difference between a hood and a community. The Hood is where the people kill, destroy, and despair is everywhere. The Community is a place of life and hope, and where the neighbors operate their own business, and have a say so, towards what goes on in their neighborhoods and can buy the "poli-trick-ions" who represent their communities. Basically, a community is a place where the people that reside there control their economics, politics and are respected and protected by the police force that they own. Since black folks don't own anything they are not respected or protected; instead they get neglected and totally disrespected. The hood is where things are hidden and a place to die of hopelessness. Again, what I am saying is nothing new, if my people don't change their patterns of thinking. They cannot and will not change the conditions of their environment. Yes, I know there are many external forces against us, but the black man and woman have always been resilient when facing obstacles. Hell, we have been facing obstacles all our lives. There comes a point where excuses cannot be used, and we have to change those things that we can, or continue to make them lame ass excuses why we can't do something. Black people were able to build vibrant communities one generation after slavery. Now in the twenty- first century we have not replicated what was done a generation after physical slavery. If we can't become economically sufficient there has to be a psychological component here, as to why we can't make the adjustment.

Power is not money, power is having the ability to influence a society: politically, mentally, economically, educationally, and environmentally.

Real power can make a difference not just for a moment, but for a lifetime. Black folks something simple as coalescing and talking to each other could be the start to making the hood a neighborhood. Something this simple could progress into forming a community. It's time to make a change, and we are the people that have to do it.

Suggestion moment: One tiny baby step black folks can take is that they can greet each other when they pass one other on the streets. Show some respect, and try to be courteous towards each other. This can dissolve some of this self-hate, and please stop all this dam mean mugging. Stop acting like you are going into a boxing ring with Iron Mike when we encounter each other. Just stop it already! Please. Remember that we are all plagued with the same illness of self-hate, and that we need an antidote of love to be restored back to the loving and caring people that we are. It is time to build each other up, and stop tearing each other down. "When I stop having compassion for another human being, then I am no longer a contributor to the human race."

~Take for an example, the self hate runs so deep that my beautiful black queens have made buying pig hair, dog hair, human hair, horse hair, rat hair and whatever other type of hair a billion dollar industry~

My beautiful black sisters: I wrote a poem about it want to hear?

Sisters in locks

India Aria said, that you are not your hair so my sister's you shouldn't care when they stop to stare, and criticize your beautiful nappy hair.

My sista's you need to de-program that Eurocentric view, and learn to love you. My dark: my caramel, my Creole, and my, light complexion vanilla sister's. My sister's you are the original creation of life. Sister's do you know, that all life came from you?

My sister's, stop polluting your beautiful bodies with all these chemicals; just so you can have an unnatural look. And stop spending your hard earned money, out of your pocket book just to have that Barbie doll look. Take a page out of your own Afro – Centric book and wear that natural look.

My sister's it is your duty as the original woman to carry your own natural beauty. Do you remember when you were told that your natural beauty was evil? And that your full lips were ugly? And your big fat butt was too big and round, and that your hair was scary?

Take a good look around because now you've got those same folks,
Who brain washed you into thinking that your natural beauty was horrific,
They're now trying to steal your hips, your lips, and your behind.
They even got you believing that you're inferior to their kind.

Sister's stop following the signs of time and utilize your own mind. Sister's you are the greatest creation ever put upon this earth, so wear that blackness for all the world to see, because your natural hair is beautiful, and it's free.

--This was written to enlighten my beautiful sister's because they are truly the greatest gift ever put upon this earth. So they need to love themselves for who they are and quit perpetrating someone else's image.

Again, I state that the sickness runs deep, and it is important that we get to the root of the problem, if we are ever going to have a chance at figuring out a solution, so that we can get well. Are we really the cursed people, because I often wonder why we do the stupid evil things we do to each other? Black folks are doing things that were unheard of doing the Black Power Movement. This **black** on **black** crime and gangster stuff; what is it good for? Does it build black folks up or tear them down? Every move black folks make, should be calculated like a chess player. They should ask this question. Is the move, I intend to make going to empower and uplift my people or will it destroy my people? Is it progress or is it regress? With everything that black folks have endured throughout their history, and what they are currently experiencing, it seems like Black folks would be a united people by now. I really don't know what it's going to take to wake up a zombie. Do you think this is a valid observation? Can the dead rise again?

There was a time where the male did have "overstanding" and not an <u>understanding.</u> They had a defined role as the disciplinary figure, the financial provider and the head of their household. The devastation of these manufactured X factors in the form of laws is evident in the Colored African American Black Negro household's. I used this term to identify the confusion we have as people. We don't even know who we are, because we don't have our own identity or an "overstanding" of it. Black people could name their selves and have one universal identity and not waiver on the name, and be proud of their heritage. This would give us a sense of ownership; it will be something we created for ourselves. This could be the starting process for changing our thinking, and bring about a change. It will give a universal connection with our brothers and sister aboard by identifying as one. Now your fight becomes our fight, can anyone visualize the power in that? How does that quote go? "So a man thinketh, he is." The point here is nothing changes unless we change are thinking!

Suggestion moment: Please black people make it mandatory for your children to read The Mis-Education of the Negro, by Carter G. Woodson. This could be the starting point for rooting out lack of knowledge of self. This could be a tool to assist in the replacing of self hate, so that they can learn to love themselves. Once that occurs there will be a total transformation in how our children interact with each other. The love that will permeate from them will have a trickledown effect on the community. There will be no stopping black folks, because they will be on the move. Also take them to African America Museums, because there's a vast array of knowledge there. When they return to their communities, their self-esteem will be altered forever. More importantly, our museums desperately need our support to stay self sustaining. If we don't tell our history, and keep it alive; then who will? Maybe the guy on the white horse will ride in and enlighten us.

The acceptable standard today for women black or white is to display their independence. There's this urgent need to show the world that they don't need a man to take care of them. They feverishly throw themselves into their work to achieve monetary success. They get their degrees, their cars, and their houses. What is missing? Come on ladies you know the song; the one by Beyoncé. (What's that song)? Oh, yeah. "All the single ladies throw your hands up." Women I see nothing wrong with being an independent woman, but to be independent from the man will lead to reducing the male role. Our role in the world will be to stand in the long lines at the sperm donor bank, and shoot our sperms in a cup for the independent women. Now she can have a baby independently without the emotional attachment of a man. That is just as unnatural as not having a father in the home. Women stop using the cliché, "I don't need a man, because I can do bad by myself." As I witnessed my daughter struggles, I realized that this cliché needs to be eliminated, because these single mothers should not have to do bad by themselves. Their struggles should be done together between a man and woman. This can also be a teachable moment for our children. We can show them that their parents can work through their struggles together. This will have an immense impact on their emotional well being as adults. If some actual though is put into this cliché, who really wants to do bad by themselves? Think about that!

Assimilation is what happened to black men, and now our black women have assimilated to the influences of the European Individual Value System? The Women Movement brought on this ideology that women are equal to men, and should have the same rights to earn and have whatever job they desired. Now that this has come to fruition, and she has secured her financial future; she wants a companion. But her purpose and vision has been tarnished, and she measures her happiness on the oppressors learned value system. The guy she seeks must have bank, so if you are that brother who attributes are: positivity, honesty, caring and all that stuff that sounds appropriate. You'll end up as the guy with the title of he's so sweet, and he's like my brother. You'll end up being her emotional garbage can. It "ain't" going to happen, for the average hard working social conscious brother if his pockets "ain't" fat. He's not going to get Mrs. Independent.

The backlash to this is the brothers who are in Corporate America, or making bank is scooped up like a hawk by the preying white women.

From a mathematical point of view the pool for black women who desire to be in a relationship with black men are shrinking; it don't matter what economic status they fall under. Women I am all for education and getting your bank right. However, these laws that the manufactured X factors have implemented has created a negative after effect. This has not benefitted the black family overall. Women's making more money is not the answer to uniting, and bringing stability and love into an unstructured family. What will? **Love** for each other, which can be challenging, because of the psychological effects of self-hate. If we can achieve love we can eliminate many of the dysfunctions that impede us from having a successful stable family. **Think about that word love, and what it means to you!**

Black men are problematic too, because instead redistributing his wealth to his black queen; he has this celebrity detachment psychosis, because he is clueless to the fact that he's only being accepted because of want he provides to the bottom line profit. The mindset of the black men who thinks he has arrived, because history told him that he could not have a fairytale snow white women. So the first opportunity presented to him, he's off and running like a thirsty bloodhound, after the first white women he smells. And now all of a sudden, he has a disdain for black women; even though his mommies a black woman. That's the identity crisis psychosis, I talked about earlier.

The system is designed to kill off so many people in this world, so they kill off the ones who are less valuable to them. Let's call it for the sake of political correctness population control. For the sake of I don't give a fxxk about being political correct; I'll call it genocide. What is the pigmentation of the people who are plagued with disease, civil unrest, famine, and institutional racism? This is bigger than not needing a black man. At this current rate black woman, you won't have to concern yourselves with where you going to find a good black man or for that sake a bad one, because you won't have a choice. He won't be around; maybe in a zoo. The zoo is where they put things after they destroy and kill it; they want a reminder of what use to be. They put things in a zoo that they don't understand; they what to study; they want to control or have made extinct. I'm a trying to paint a broader picture, to enlighten and bring light to what is esoteric. My people are perishing because of the foolish things they've been taught, which are causing their own demise.

The pools of eligible fathers are shrinking due to the limited job opportunities in the local market, and uneducated kids grow up to be uneducated adults. What I would like to bring to the light is that our babies are not prepared to compete in a global market in this current education system. Our children are being program to work, so they are not motivated to become entrepreneurs, inventors, computer application designers, doctors, lawyers, scientist, and the other vocations that will transfer into the twenty first century global economy. Why are black folks still allowing (them) the school system to continue to produce and send their precious children to these warehouses called schools, preparing them to become a commodity that's traded on Wall Street?

Black children are pawns to these X factors to produce more prison, based on the imprisonment of black boys, girls and immigrants. It is time to stop bickering and fighting about trivial things that can be worked out; there's bigger fish to fry. As long as they can divert the people from the important issues in our communities, they will have no resistance in completing their mission of genocide. How do you kill off a group of people? Deny resources and the reproduction of life, and you take those significant productive years of a man's life between the ages of 18-25. What ages are young black men being killed off? They are being killed by the hands of the oppressor, and by the hands of the people who are oppressed and look like them. The Judiciary System and the Child Support Enforcement Agency are locking brothers up for any and everything, because evidence and facts don't matter when you're poor and black. They are locking our black asses up for having babies and building more private jails for us. This is one of many examples of the subtle methods that they use to eliminate and annihilate the black family. They are doing it without much resistance from the black community. As matter of fact, the black's are assisting in their own annihilation. Think about this my strong black women who don't need a man. If all the black men are wiped out, how will you procreate? Next it will be you. Kill the head and the body will die. When are we going to have that spiritual awakening, unite and come out of that zombie state of non-existence? Look back to our history, because the solution is found there. Black people need to get back to the time when they produce things and use their education for upward mobility for the benefit of their people. Yes, they stole and profited off black folks labor& knowledge to produce their generational wealth. My point is black people did not succumb to the devices that the oppressor used to try to destroy them in the past. Why can't we overcome these same oppressors today? With less it seems like black people had more, and now with the appearance of having more; collectively we have less. Overall, economically as a people we have made a 360.

This is much more than not needing a man, my sisters who are just as lost as the black man. Sisters it's about how are we going to get out of this bondage of self-destruction so we can save us from ourselves. How will black people survive without each other? It will not be humanly possible for them to survive, and if they don't get their heads out of that dark place where the sun don't shine. It won't be too long before they find themselves taking the chains off their minds, and putting them back on their ankles. We cannot continue to be like two lost ships wandering at sea without a destination. Black people have to find their way back to the land of love, so they can prepare a future for their babies and the generations to come. Black folks get out of the delusional state of mind that somebody on a white horse or that somebody going descend from the sky to save us; it has not happened in all these centuries. Black folks have become come too dam religious, scriptures quoting, and bible carrying, to solve anything that ails their communities. These scriptures are their go to scriptures, and if you like you can go to them too, Ephesians 4: Mark 8:31 2 Timothy 2:12. Basically it is telling them to have patience with thy enemy, and remain humble and loving. That's definitely black folks, because they have been patient for over 500 years, and they are very humble. They not only adore their oppressors, they praise and revere their oppressor.

Black folks are without a doubt loyal and obedient to Jesus. Just keep on waiting because help is coming; we might not know when he's coming but he's always on time. Hold on the struggle won't last always just wait on the lord, and he will see you through all your troubles. He will make your enemy your foot stool, all you got to do is don't give up now, and wait on the lord Jesus Christ your savior. Can I get an Amen? The church begins to shout and dance. Well, we are going to keeping on waiting to somebody come and save us from our pain suffering. The mind set of suffering has been indoctrinated in their minds for so long that they have come to believe a lie to be the truth, and that they can't do it for themselves, because there's a savior coming to save them from all the oppression and aguish bestowed upon them. Just keep allowing the following: injustices, killings, unequal education, and health care disparities. We continue to be willing participants in our own demise.

Suggestion moment: Take the ego and pride out of the churches, and bring all the thousands of ineffective churches that are on every street corner next to the liquor stores and crack houses, and build one big institution. Those ministers who have less than three hundred members can hold some type of position; but it may not be in the same capacity that they once held. Create a board where the business minded, social minded, and of course the preacher to bring forth the word on Sunday. Are you getting the vision people? Now God's word can begin to manifest in the people because their conditions will change mentally, spiritually, and financially. Now a difference for the multitude of people can be made, and not just for members of the church. By uniting the church it becomes the change agent for all the people from the East, West, South, and North. The church can now be the pillar in the four corners of the city to build up a nation of people. Can anyone see the vision? How can the people come together when there is division amongst us? The churches must organize and unite the people (Matthew 5:16).

History has since been reversed due to numerous changes in man laws, and the strong will of men to protect their women and assume their roles as father has been effected. Their roles have been redefined so there's a dire need for a dialogue to ask why black men are vanishing from the world and from their homes. Are these men being driven out by unseen and seen variables that desire a certain outcome, which is to create division amongst them? United we fall, and divided we will stand. Oh, the tears I cry for the state of mind of my people. **I wrote a poem about want to hear:**

Tears I Cry

Oh, the tears that I cry for the state of mind of my people. Oh, the tears I cry for babies having babies, and babies without fathers and

fathers without fathers. Oh, the tears I cry for the racism that cripples and strangles the mind of my people. Oh, the tears that I cry for the modern day slavery disguised as justice. Oh, the tears that I cry for the institutionalizing of my brothers and sisters. Oh, the tears that I cry for self –destruction of my people.

Oh, the tears that I cry for the lack of self-knowledge; instead of my young brothers standing on the street corners they should be in college seeking knowledge. Oh, the tears that I cry for the lack of leadership in my community or shall I say our community. Oh, tears that I cry for the banking institutions that takes, takes, takes and gives nothing in return but false hope things to be desired.

Oh, my tears of thee the land of modern day slavery.

Oh, the tears that I cry when I see my bothers with their heads down in despair like they just don't care. They have lost hope and now they are standing on the corner selling dope.

Oh, the tears I cry when I see my young sister selling their minds body and soul and for what? For a brother standing on the street corners with a neck full of gold, and that stuff is getting old it is time for the real story to be told. How we produce the fruit of this land and yet we're still considered 3/5 of a man. Oh, these are the tears that I cry for the state of mind of my people.

CHAPTER 2
How it all began?

Let's start this journey with the writer and how this story began.

My Family Origin:

Some historians and philosophers and family therapist believe that searching your past will propel an individual to unveil their mask, and become that person they are capable of becoming. As I began to reflect upon my family dynamics, there were these roaring of emotions that began stirring inside of me. I felt fearful, guilty, ashamed, judgmental, inadequate, helpless, and sad. And a plethora of other emotions, that will be explored later in the purging of myself. Here is my lineage from my prospective and knowledge I obtain from my dad and ancestors.

Part I. How it all began:

Chuck and Lucinda gave birth to four sons in Palestine, Arkansas. George was born in 1909, and Nat - Jan 20, 1910; YZ was born November 12, 1915. Nat he would wed Maple Lee Miller. That union gave birth to Bob on March 12, (1935) He had a sister from this union René who was born in 8/26/ 1936

Bob would wed and have a son name Bob who was tragically killed by an automobile in 1971. **Bob** married La' sometime during the sixties

Three children would come from this union of Bob and La'. 1. La' was born June 13, 1956 {2. Lee. Sept 22, 1957, and died of internal bleeding in 1996 after being beaten by assailants in the neighborhood where he grew up at. Lee who was known as Jimbo was a nice guy, and always wanted to help and please others. He would hang out with the guys where he grew up, but the problem was that these guys never grew up outside the walls of the project. He thought that because he grew up with these guys that they were his friends, but they were not his friends. Jimbo was trusting and a loving brother. This may have been his demise trusting others too much. Jim worked the same job since high school, and like nice clothes, music, and playing the boggles. I miss my brothers so much. 3. Pork was born March 9, 1962. His was called "Pork" by his family and friends because of how his physically appearance. Soon thereafter, Bob got involved with my mom Tee.

Bob met Tee who had five children already from a previous marriage by Butch: 1. {James Aug 27, 1949}2. {Lane Dec 3, 1950} 3. {Butch March 29, 1952}4. {Junkie J March 31, 1960} 5. {Tamari June 4, 1962}

Shortly, thereafter, Action was born who would later be called Action Jackson in 1984, after an official name change to his father name Bob. Out of this relationship my mom and dad (**Bob and Tee) there came three children: Bob 8/15/1963,Bit 10/16/1964 and the baby boy Jay born 9/6/1966.**

My personal experiences:

I have some fun memories growing up. The one I remember vividly is when my dad rented a mobile home to travel to see grand-dad in Arkansas. We would go almost every year, but that year was special because all the children went. Let me be more specific, when I say all the children this included dads' children from La, and the three of the children from my mother, Tee, and the three which included me that dad had before he got with mother sometime in 1962. It was a crazy trip with so many people including my cousin Anthony and his wife and daughter. It makes me chuckle now when I think of all the disagreements that took place and the confusion that went on. Yet, we managed to still have fun. I also can recall my older brothers James and Bob (who we called Butch). They were not around very much and I later found out why. To this day, I do not know why he was called Butch, everyone called him Butch; even mom. Another memory that stands out is imitating the Jackson Five; it was T, our three neighbors, and I. We would practice for hours, because we were determined to appear on the Gene Carroll show. Today the show would probably be the equivalence to the American Idol, but on the local level in Detroit, Michigan. We eventually, got our chance to actually audition to appear on the Gene Carroll show.

I remember a school mate who was robbed and killed, and every time I hear the Whispers song "Living together in Sin" it reminds me an innocent life that was stolen through hatred and violence. Not knowing that the death experience would resurface into my own life years later. That is when I began to look at the world through different lenses. One of the memories I would like to do away with is the dreadful memory of the deaths of my three brothers. Especially, James because I was the last person to see him alive the night he was <u>murdered.</u> Well, all their deaths were equally devastating, but James death I had terrible nightmares for years.

During this point in my life after the murder of James I decided to reflect upon my life, and at that moment I knew I had to make a change from what I was doing. One day in the summer of 1981, I just starting walking aimlessly and I ended up at The Army Recruitment office on Lee drive. I joined the Army on July 14, 1981. I dropped out of high school my last year, and joined the Army at the tender age of seventeen. I needed to get away from my environment and I needed some structure in my life.

The military is a blessing and a curse, because I took that same behavior that I had in the street into the military. I fell victim to my behavior and got involved with the same type of people I was trying to escape from. What I realized was that I couldn't escape from myself, and that I had to change my way of thinking.

Transitioning to a brighter note, I also can recall all the fun I had as child: playing on the salt mountains, climbing tall trees, building clubhouses, catching grasshoppers, playing marbles building go- carts, and playing hide go seek. I am not going to mention the other hide go seek game we played with the girls. There were so many fond memories back then. We played marbles, made slingshots guns, played football and baseball in the parks. My mom would make us submarine sandwiches to take to the swimming pool. We were the rare family that had lunch, and that made me feel important. That made us popular with the swimming pool gang. I was the leader of the SWAT team. There was a television show that came on television called S.W.A.T. and my brother Jay, Casper, and I would jump garages and act like we were really catching the bad guys. Yes, those were the days. Where your neighbor know you, and would look out for you like family. Whatever happened to those good old days?

Relationship with Parents:

Mother, (Tee March 1933-2004) I was able to confide in her when I was going through things, but it was always that surface type sharing. However, it was never that catharsis type moment. Mom was a caring and loving individual who would give the shirt off her back. However, she was an enabler too. She would often over protect us, and sometime when daddy wanted to discipline us, mom would intervene. Mom was a stay-at-home mother, she never work, but the way I see it raising eight rambunctious children was more than work. Mom died on May 2, 2004, at 5:08 am, and after that something dramatically changed in me. During my mom's home going, I can vividly recall the words of the pastor, "if you loved your mother then let her life and love continue to live in you." I began to honor my mother dying words. She asks me to finish school, and I promised her I would. I was driven to complete my undergraduate degree, and I swear there were times when I was not motivated to honor her wishes. There were times when I felt my mother's presence, and it gave me the motivation and courage to continue. I miss her so very much to this day; there was so much I could have done to make her quality of life better.

Dad, (Bob was born March 12, 1935) Dad was a man above men. He worked very hard and believed that a man responsibility was to provide for his family financially. My dad parenting style was authoritarian; it was certainly not parallel to mom's parenting style. Her style was a hybrid between permissive and authoritative, because if you took her there she would go there with you, but you really would have to get on her very last nerve. Which I am sure I did on more than one occasion. I say that, to say this; all and all I would not trade my child hood experiences for anything, because I never wanted for anything while growing up as a child. There was some pain, but all my good days out weighted my bad days. I had a father who had to work two jobs, so I never saw him much doing the day. My dad and mom would often argue about him being in the streets when he was not working, and about how he disciplined us. As I began to mature into adolescence, I saw things clearer about what was really going on in my family structure. There were definitely some dysfunctional things going on in my family, but I will leave it at that for now. More will be revealed in my analysis. I used to be so angry and rebellious towards my father. I blamed everyone for my problems but me. Today, I do not blame dad for my unwise choices in life. Today we tell each other that we love one another and it's heartfelt. Man... God, sobriety and maturity can change a person.

Siblings Relationship:

Siblings, I really cannot say much about the relationships with my brother and sisters. The older brothers and sisters were not present much. We had sibling conflict, but our conflict went beyond what is considered normal, and I will leave it at that. Well, if I was to compare the 1960's to 2015, maybe my family was not so bad. I can say without a doubt that dysfunction definitely played a role in my life. I can only describe this section as disassociation and detachment. There was an enormous amount of anger among my siblings. The family probably should have gotten some professional help to explore this sibling situation.

During that time people in my community just didn't talk about what went on inside their household in a public forum; like we do today. I am convinced that my dysfunctional family has had an effect on my mental state, and some of my decisions I have made in my life. Nevertheless, the choices I made as an adult has nothing to do with my parents or my siblings. It had to do with lack of discipline, and not wanting to listen to my elders who had experienced my life struggles already. My way of thinking was irrational. It was like trying to travel to a destination, and my parents and the elders who have travelled that destination multiple times, but I am telling them how to get there and I have never been there. I am travelling I-71 South, trying to get to Detroit, it "ain't" possible and I will never get to Detroit. I continue to travel my own path until God said, "enough of doing it your way, it's time to do my way." He finally woke me up one day, and made me realize that I had to change my direction or I was heading nowhere fast.

Self Analysis:

Reflecting on my early childhood and adolescence, I can see how not having a true connection with my siblings, and why I struggled with being a loving and caring person in my intimate and my friendships. This is why I probably shared my surface emotions, and not the deep stuff I needed to share with my family and friends. I can see where Virginia Satir's therapeutic method can be beneficial for me in terms of gut wrenching communicating. Furthermore, I do believe there may have been some identity crisis too, being the six of twelve children in a non-nuclear family structure. I was the oldest child in my nuclear family of K and Jay, and in my extended family I was the middle child. Therefore, I do believe I suffered from what Adler called, "being squeezed out." I can now comprehend why had problems trusting people, and not wanting to get emotionally attached. Thus, causing problems in my relationships, and the reason why I was angry. I believe the anger manifested when I lost my second brother, in 1980. And then had to bury him on my birthday. Through my trials and tribulations, I believe my epiphany came when my mom died. That is when I had that resurgence or that spiritual awakening to become a better person. I realized that life was for the living, and I was going to live, I was going to be that person God wanted me to be. Finally, I realized that my anger issues were spurred on by the deaths of my brothers and it was a defense mechanism that I used to avoid dealing with my emotions. I was spiritually and mentally bankrupted. Furthermore, I am now aware that my self-destructive behavior had caused a tremendous amount of unhealthy transference to my family.

Structural Therapy Approaches of Psychopathology:

Murray Bowen (1913-1990) He believed that emotional illness occurred when individuals are unable to adequately differentiate themselves from their families of origin. **Differentiation of self** is the ability to be emotionally controlled while remaining within the emotional intensity of one's family (Prochaska and Norcross 2010). He said rather than resolve triangles through self-differentiation, most people use **emotional cutoff.** This term I identified with, because I saw a relationship in my life like what he described as denial and isolation of problems when living close to parents, or physically running away, or a combination of the two. I was definitely in denial and distant from my family, because I felt there was never that family unity, so I sought other means of being connected to something, and I did run away several times, which I failed to mention previously.

Virginia Satir (-1988) Catharsis she combined systemic theory with ego, psychology, and Gestalt theory. Satir agreed that troubled families need to communicate clearly. Most troubled families have difficulties in communicating their feelings directly. If they cannot be clear about their feeling towards each other, they certainly would be more likely to be ambiguous rules for relating. Satir's (1967, 1972; Satir& Baldwin, 1983; Satir, Stachowiak, &Taschman, 1977) approach to systemic work, therefore, accord more importance when helping families express their emotions and thereby change the rules that prohibit emotional relating. Her theory on communicating, was the problem that kept my family so distant to one another. We just did not know how to relate to one other in a healthy productive way. Therefore, I just avoided the whole scene of trying to relate to my family. I can see the results of that today in my family.

Salvador Minuchin (1922-) disengaged family- In the disengaged family, there is little or no contact between family members. There is a relative absence of healthy structure, order, or authority. Ties between family members are weak or nonexistent. The overall impression of a disengaged family is distance and disconnect (Prochaska and Norcross 2010).

CHAPTER 3

Sex "ain't" Love & Love "ain't" sex

I guess sex is a great way to start a conversation about having babies. I had my first child at the age of twenty three, and it was a boy. I thought this was going to be the turning point in my life. I had a boy, and I thought I would be able to mold him into a better version of me, and to guide him on how to make better choices, because I certainly was all too familiar with making unwise choices, so I was going to imbue into him the opposite of what my crazy experiences were. I was going to teach my baby boy how to use his brain to navigate through this journey called life. I was going to teach him how to be a man, and do all those things men do. Whatever that is? Of course none of this would transpire, because if it did the title of this book would have a different name. Life is truly a miracle and very precious; however, somehow the great wonder of creating a life had turn out to be a major crisis for me.

My five minutes of pleasure has manifested into a life time of pain in the worst imaginable way. The birth of my child would turn out like a Shakespeare tragedy. I want to inform the readers that there is a difference between sex and love. The era that I grew up in, it was a symbol of manhood to go back on the block and tell your homeboys how many women you had conquered with your pulsating manhood. It was like a badge of honor and acceptance into manhood to knock a piece of meat, because that is how I viewed women as something to consume and devour. The more women I persuaded to drop their panties the more respect my boys had for me. I became a legend in my own mind. The more I hunted the better I got, and after perfecting my skills. I became a natural at emotionally scarring and taking, giving nothing in return. I though all I had to offer a woman was my phallus, but I discovered that there is more to being a man than keeping a woman in the prone position. We need to make love to each other minds and not just our physical body. In a healthy relationship a man feeds his woman mind, and the woman feeds her man's mind. This sets the stage for them to go beyond their natural potential and excel in God's supernatural potential. While in church a woman said this: "God has impregnated every woman with a seed of destiny, and in order to give birth to her true purpose, a loving man of God will have to align himself with her to assist her in giving birth to her true destiny". Men and women when you call yourselves hooking up with your significant other make sure you are able to feed each other with these five essential elements: **Physical, emotional, mental, spiritual and financial**

Women and men there is a difference between sex and love, because sex "ain't" love and love "ain't" sex. See when performing sex it was just an act being performed: in the bedroom, in the car, behind a dumpster, behind a garage, in a garage, inside a dressing room at a busy shopping mall, under the blankets on the beach. Well, you get the picture. I was always thinking below the waist and that's where my thought process ended. I was always thinking with my little head and not my big head, above my shoulders. Women have paid a hell of an emotional price because of me sticking my dick everywhere without a care. **I wrote a poem about it want to hear it?**

Mr. Dick

The D' stands for Mr. Dick, because he's not about getting emotionally involved or about having a long term relationship. He'll let you know off the rip, that he only thinks below the hip so don't think about having a long term relationship.

Women if you are looking for Mr. Right, this is the time to run and take flight, because Mr. Dick is not that guy, because he only wants to stay the night. Don't you dare get attached to Mr. D' because the next girl that comes along Mr. Dick will be long gone, and you'll find yourself dick-less and home alone.

Mr D' is not disrespectful he's just a straight shooter, and he only shoots from the hip. Women if you are lonely and vulnerable, you had better be aware, because Mr. Dick just doesn't care, so if you need a good fuck call Mr. Dick and he'll be right there, and like always without a care.

The only setback about Mr. Dick is that because of his promiscuous ways it would also be his downfall; it has become a curse rather than a pleasure. This I-don't- care attitude has lead Mr. Dick into countless pitfalls, heartaches, and pain. Mr. Dick has not been able to stay and maintain healthy loving relationships. You see Mr. Dick don't think, he acts first and thinks later. His I-don't-care mentality has cost him financial woes, and caused him to lose people who wanted to love him. Mr. Dick has gotten older, and he can't put out like he once did. He is no longer the man he used to be, and his performance is limited, at best. The Dick has left him lonely and holding on to the memories of what could have been. The power of Mr. Dick can be a good thing if it is used for the right purpose, and not for my self seeking pleasure. Men, respect Mr. Dick and don't give it to any and everybody, because it could lead to your own demise. These are words from the wise, so take these words and don't think twice.

When I love a woman it is an act performed outside the bedroom by my external actions, and it has nothing to do with putting my pulsating manhood in your secret place. Women you have to distinguish between the two, because you can't find love if it's not there. I guess it was something embedded in me during that time in my life. There was something besides immaturity that perpetuated this type of behavior towards women. I did not have the mental capacity to comprehend that this was not normal behavior. Or was it? It certainly appeared normal in the environment where I came from. Maybe there is an underlying issue that I am not consciously aware of when it comes to women and my sexual desires.

I was not astute in the area of communicating, because I came from a family where communication came in the form of: we talked loud at each other, we out talked and over talked each other and we talked at rather than to each other. I did not learn about effective communication until later in life, and sometimes I still fall short in that area. I took a class in college called effective communication, and it was suggested that when a person communicates, specific elements needed to be involved.

The first thing I was taught was to speak directly to the person whom I am addressing. Secondly, there must be a two way engagement to have conversation. The speaking who is the sender of the message, and on the other end of the message there must be a receiver of the message. The receivers then clarify by rephrasing the sender message. This informs the sender that the receiver was listening to the message, and clarifies what the receiver interpreted. The final stage would be communication where the two people are engaging in a dialogue. The elements should contain the following: speak- clarify- listen – respond- and engage in what was communicated; effective communication should be our goal. I know it is easier said than done; especially when pride and emotions are involved.

As some of us know, we can read a million self-help books and there's a plethora of material out there on any subject desired, depending on which subject one would like to explore. There are books on communication, relationships, marriages, and if you can name it you can find it. The catch here is that this can apply to other areas of our lives. Nevertheless, if this information is not being applied into our lives it will not make a difference in our lives. I am not claiming to be an expert. I just want people know if we try, we can to do better, and become well-adjusted both socially and culturally. When we do those things, they will transfer to our children. My spin on advice is this, people are going to do what they want, but the people who are the exception are the few that do listen. They are the ones that usually don't fall so hard, and if and when they do they have a soft cushion of good advice to break their fall. We cannot solve any of our problems if we do not acknowledge that there is a problem. Black parents, we got some problems that we need to put under a magnifying glass to examine our maladies. Yes other ethnic groups have their disorders too, but the media and their wealth offers the luxury of not having the bull's eye on their back. Right now I am not addressing them, because they have their safety net of the law and white privilege on their side. Black folks do not have those privileges. That's why we are in this constant whirlwind of upheaval and struggle. It is like accepting being on a bad diet; we know the stuff is bad for us. We know we got to replace the bad stuff with something good. The problem is we don't know what's good for us. If we continue to put the spiritual, physical and the mental bad stuff in us, we are going to get sicker. Parents, community churches, and families, it is time to get healthy, so we can live and not die.

Women from a male perspective I am only going to do what you allow me to do, so early on, in the getting-to-know-you process of building a relationship. I am going to test the boundaries. Unfortunately, because of the DNA make-up of the female, she allows her maternal nurturing instincts to control her emotions. Therefore, only acting on her heart strings and not on the action of the man; which usually results in sleeping with the guy before a relationship is established. (Self worth female): Dam ladies at least take the time to learn where he lives, work, and his real name before you give up the goods. My dad would say the, "longest distance from A to B is from the heart to the brain". (Self worth male): For men our self worth is in the delusion of sex. Why? Because that is the only area that we can control, and dominant and makes us feel like we got some value. It inflates our male ego. We cannot control our community, families, business, wealth, and our resources are limited.

We have one thing that they have not taken from us yet, and that is our false sense of manhood, which is that tool in our pants. I don't know, this shit might have something do with them chopping off our penis doing those dark days in our history. There may be some sort of correlation to why we place such high esteem in our dicks. The powers that be have always had a fascination with the Blackman's dick. They have build monuments and statues of the Blackman's Phallus. I've digressed. Where was I? Sorry, you have to do some research on that topic. I "ain't" going there, that's another book and conversation.

Women the measurement and the standards you set will be the moral compass that guides the males pulsating manhood. Ladies let me put it to you as plainly as possible concerning how men think. Most of us with the exception of a few are only going to put out the minimum requirements. Women if you want queen-like treatment, you better have some queen-like qualities and standards. Women what's your self-worth? That is something I nor any other man can give you. If you act like a queen you get treated like a queen, and if you act like a hoe you get treated like a ten dollar hoe, and that's the harsh reality of this game. Women how do you treat yourself? Another thing don't let no man tell you your standards are too high, who in the fuck is he to tell you how you deserve to be treated. Women you have to understand that you deserve to be treated with the utmost respect. Unfortunately, that experience often times come by the way of pain and heartache before you realize you deserve better. To my brothers who consider themselves players, I'm going to hit you with a dose of reality. While you are out there playing, and not being accountable for your children. Real talk men, if you are not there for your daughters' you will have the experience that I witness. You will feel the pain of seeing your precious daughter endure the pain and suffering of her bad choices from dog-ass men like you once were, and if you are not there for your boys they will become those men who will inflict suffering upon the daughters.

Muhammad Ali Advice to his daughter: Daughter everything that God made valuable is covered and hard to get to. Where do you find diamonds? Deep down in the ground, covered and protected. Where do find pearls? Deep down at the bottom of the ocean, covered and protected in a beautiful shell. Where do you find gold? Way down deep down in the mine covered over with layers and layers of rock. You've got to work hard to get them. He looked at his daughter with serious eyes. "Your body is sacred. You're far more precious than diamonds and pearl, and you should be covered too.

The way you treat yourself, sets the criteria for how others will treat you. Women don't compromise your dignity and respect. Women and men both deserve respect, so let's make an effort to respect each other. This will save us from future heart aches and pain, and it will definitely have an enormous impact on our children. This is reinforcing positive imagery that black men and women do not have to be at arms with each other, and that they can resolve their differences in a loving and caring way. This negates those negative imagines shown in the media outlets that black folks are only about violence and drama.

Women stop! Thinking that you going to love a man until he loves you back. Men just don't operate like that. Sorry, but get out of that fantasy world and wake up. Women don't tolerant under any circumstances allowing a man to disrespect you, and definitely don't let him think that it's cool to hit you. When he does that he has self- esteem issues and he wants to control and dominant you. The outcome is never a good one. Open those eyes and ears and take some advice from the seasoned women and men of the community. Young women if you are dropping babies like rabbits, and having them by every man that tells you he loves you, you might want to seek help from somebody; maybe the big boss man upstairs himself.

Now I am not proud of my acts of selfishness and self indulgence, but I must paint the picture of my mind frame during this matriculation into manhood. Nevertheless, when I was out there hunting my prey, I became victim to my own self destructive behaviors, and now I am reaping the repercussion of my own narcissism.

Fast-forward into the now: here's some advice for the brothers who are still out there chasing that pussy and leaving a trail of emotionally scarred women. I'm telling you it's like a drug you want more and more, and you will never be satisfied with just one. And years later you are going to wake up old and gray, and realize a day late and a dollar short that there's no one there for you. You're all alone by yourself and that thing between your legs that offered that false power and control has ceased to operate. Now all you have is the memories of the past trails of pain you've caused women. Now you wish that you could turn back the hands of time, and dry up the flooded rivers of tears from those emotionally scarred women.

I had a catharsis moment. With all this talking about self-worth and looking in the mirror, I actually discovered some truth about myself. The thought came to my mind in regards to one of the ladies I was involved with. She told me that I wanted love on my terms. With that thought in mind, it got the wheels turning in my mind; why I could not sustain a healthy relationship? Some of these women I dated had all the qualities that I wanted. They were intelligent; they were career oriented; they were involved in charitable organizations; they contributed to their communities, and they gave to me more love than I deserved.

What I discovered about myself and relationship was this. When it came to loving me and having this elusive self worth; I had none. I discovered that I was this frighten little boy who believed he didn't deserve to be loved by such beautiful, talented, and caring women, so I would find ways to sabotage these relationships. I knew by having more than one woman and not committing to either woman that it would catch up with me. Eventually, it always did. Taking these women along on this emotional rollercoaster ride that I was on, would prove to be a dangerous game. I was stabbed by one of those loving and caring women. God stepped in again! These women did not deserve this emotional anguish by this boy imitating a man. I had to stop thinking with my phallus; even if these women were throwing their womanhood right in my hands. I could not stop I was powerless over the pussy. If God descended from heaven to have a one on one with me and gave me a choice between being faithful to woman and becoming a miserable sick old man. I would probably ask God could he come back in a few days, and I'll give him a decision later. He'll probably punish me for that, and I'll probably end up at McDonalds drinking coffee early in the morning and staying late in the evening with the other lonely old bastards.

This promiscuous behavior affected my mental stability. When I became spiritually conscience this behavior ate at the core of my soul, because now I knew morally that this behavior was not acceptable to God. I had to seek something to numb the pain from the pain of the pain I was causing myself and others. This behavior was starting to have an adverse effect on me. Have you ever been in situation where you did not want to do something? You had that gut feeling but you continue to do it, knowing that the outcome would not be a positive one. But because of my drinking thinking, I would commit these acts over and over again. Getting the same result; I think some guy named Einstein called this insanity. When you do the same thing over and over again and you are expecting a different result, but have not done anything to have a different outcome. I don't know if it is true, but have you heard that every person a woman or man sleeps with becomes a part of their spirit and mind. Well if there's any validity to that, then I can see the correlation as to why I have not been able to maintain and stay in a committed relationship. I am confused, because I have all these dam people inside of me. Well, I will make a heck of a specimen. All these spirits inside of my mind they are confused as hell and don't know what to do. The positive thing out of all of this madness is when I die; there will be a team of scientists who will be gainfully employed studying my brains. My desire to seek sexual pleasure rather than a healthy committed relationship needs to be examined by a specialist or someone who is highly trained. Why am I so fearful of a commitment? Women if I don't get an answered to this question there will be hell for you to pay, and I will continue to cause havoc in your lives. This is real talk!

My life would take a turn for the worse. I had no inkling to what was going to transpire on that hot summer day in Detroit. Had I known, I would have definitely taken an alternate route. It all began with my buddy Kenny Wayne, and I challenging each other to see how many girls numbers we could get. This life changing journey began on Eight Mile to the Village. We were returning from our boy Tim's house, and we was feeling good off that cheap rot gut MD/20/20 wine we had consumed voraciously. We had not gotten any numbers on our travels to Tim's house because we had got distracted with the other challenge of stealing wine, which superseded the former challenge of getting girls numbers.

This challenge would turn out to be one of the most difficult battles I would face, and it would lead to a life of bad choices, set ups and setbacks. My road dog and I would go into each store that crossed our paths and five finger discount a bottle of wine. If my memory serves me correctly, our wine of choice was Ice Tea and Mad Dog. As I reflect on the name Mad Dog, it was the very symbol of how and what my life would become mad and out of control. Kenny Wayne hollered out to me, from behind because I was the one in front on our ten speed bikes that we had purchased that summer. "Hey, man there's one." As if this living human soul with emotions, and a heart beat was some type of animal we were hunting for our human survival. Because he had spotted her first and my consumption of mad dog had decreased my motor skills, he sped up to try to get her number before I had a chance. His attempt led to rejection. "Let me show you how a true player gets down for his crown." "Step back boy, I'm going teach you a thing or two about this pimpin game."

I rode over to her, to spit my sweet nothings in her ear, and gave her my bullshit lines. "Hi. Why are you walking girl?" "You too dam fine to be walking." "Hi, girl you must exercise a lot, because you have been running through my mind all day." She continues to walk. "You don't mind if I put my sun glasses on do you, because you're blinding me with all that beauty?" I really wanted to say her ass, because that what was really blinding me. "Hey, girl can I spend some time, because you're fine as wine?" She responded, "That is so whack, you can't come up with a better line than that?" "No! But my whack ass lines got you smiling, and you stop walking and you're talking to me."

"You didn't give that other guy a shot, so there got to be something about a brother you like." Let's cut the small talk and tell me your name and give me those seven digits. "My name is Danita and my number is 769-453", and what the last number foxy mama?" "You have to figure it out", so I write her number inside the cover of some matches, that I found in my green polo shirt pocket. All right I'll be talking to you later, as I'm riding off, she yells one."

This phone number would prove to be detrimental to my mental, spiritual, and physical well being. This encounter would have a lasting impact on several people lives in an unforgettable way. The player thought he was playing, but in the end it would be the player getting played. My boy as we are riding off, he's giving me my high fives, "man you the man." "Yeah, don't you forget that boy, if you want to know something come to your papa boy?" "Now go into the store and get the next one, "man you get the girl and I got to steal the wine?" "Yep, it's your turn anyway KW."

It would only take a few phone calls, and after that it was on and poppin. I went H-Town on her, and I was knocking those boots. Most of the time I would go over her house, which her mom did not mind. That should have been a **red flag** for me. I was not working and did not even have a car, and her mom would buy me beer. I was in heaven. I had a hot pussy and a cold beer waiting for me, because that all I cared about. I had no aspirations, inspirations or any expectations for my life. I had no love for another human being; maybe I pretended to. I was a self-serving selfish you-know-what. I wanted what I wanted, when I wanted. If I hadn't been under the influence of that sweet Lucy,(that's what my dad calls alcohol) I would have noticed that this was not a normal situation for a young man and young woman to be in. During those limited moments of clarity, which were few and far between, I began to notice that her mom controlled every facet of her life. There were no people coming to visit them and her mom never talk about her father, and I never saw her father come around. The warning signs were all there, but I did not see them at the time because I had a hot pussy and a cold beer waiting on me when I got there. See I didn't have a whole lot of ambition or expectations for myself or for that matter, anyone else. I would later discover that fundamentally things were dysfunctional in that house hold. This information would come a dollar short and day late. (Another one of my dad's adages) I would fall victim to their irrational thinking and of my own.

They created their own reality; it was sort of like when I was drunk I had my own distorted reality too. Next thing I know, about a month later, she was telling me, "I got something I need to tell you." Now in my irrational thinking, I'm thinking she was about to give me my get out of jail for free pass. That she wanted to release me from this mental bondage, which would be a blessing in disguise. Nope, I wouldn't be that fortunate. In her condescending way; her lips smacking, and her eyes looking like they were about to pop out of her forehead. "I'm having a baby." My head felt like it had grown twice the size of her forehead, and it felt like my head was about to explode. I was speechless, it felt like the world had stop turning on its axis. After that I could not hear, see or smell all my senses had went into a black hole and vanished. I began to stutter to get my words out, "What Wha Wha …What you going to do?" For those who have taken the efforts to read this book here are some suggestions from my personal experiences.

When two individual create a life, it is an absolute miracle because the process of life itself is a miracle, so all life is precious and a special gift from God. Here are a few pointers: Please men, adhere to my suggestions before bringing a life into this world. Plan parenthood, be in a relationship, and have a plan of action for that child's life. Most importantly, try to have an ideal of the mental state of mind of the person you decide to create a life with. Again, women remember sex "ain't "love & love" "ain't" sex. Don't think because you give a man a baby all sudden he's going to be ready or even capable of being a dad. He is not going to suddenly transform into Dr. Huxtable, that outstanding father Bill Cosby played on television; if it is not in his DNA.

My situation absolutely did not parallel the Huxtables family. It was more compatible to nightmare on Elm Street. I do not blame the mother of my child at all; it is not about blaming anyone for my choices. This is about me being a father to my son. I chose to have sex with this woman no one forced me to stick my pole in her hole. I was not that ignorant not to know that if you have unprotected sex there is a possibility of making a baby. As I reflect, sex was the only activity we did together. And nine times out of ten when sex was acted out in the bedroom, I was pissy drunk. Well, that's what I get for sticking my dick everywhere. I got a baby mama who is controlled by her mother. I can only imagine what my poor little baby went through. He must have gone through some struggles living with two angry women and no father or a positive male role model.

I do not think being economically disadvantaged gives one an excuse to be a bad parent; however, I do believe not trying to improve your conditions in life does, so that your children can have choices. This may make a parent eligible as a candidate for being an unskilled parent. That is more politically correct than saying a bad parent. Whatever, termed used bad or unskilled, there should have been something put in place like parenting classes, interpersonal skills classes, and job preparation. Those should have been one of the requirements for her receiving welfare for eighteen years, and now I am responsible for paying that money back. I think these suggestions can improve the lives of the mother; thus making the child's life better. If the mother is spiritually, mentally, and physically well rounded, this makes for a happy mom. When mom is happy everyone is happy.

There is nothing wrong with being poor because the bible said, "For you have the poor with you always."(Matt 26:11) But wanting to stay poor and being ignorant is where I see a problem. I did not understand at the time why Danita did not have a desire to work and get a place of her own. Why did she stay on welfare for eighteen years? Money does not necessary make a person the Huxtable family, but it does provide the family more options and opportunities to make choices for their family. Poverty diminishes an individual's hope and aspiration. Dr. Martin Luther King said, "The curse of poverty has no justification in our age. It is socially as cruel and blind as the practice of cannibalism at the dawn of civilization, when men ate each other because they had not yet learned to take food from the soil or to consume the abundant animal life around them. The time has come for us to civilize ourselves by the total, direct and immediate abolition of poverty."

What is hope? Hope for me is an opportunity to nurture and raise my child and provide him with the tools needed to navigate through the rough seas of life, and help provide him the navigation skills to make it safely to shore. Hope for me is to one day hug my child who is now a grown man. Hope for me is to live to see my son's mother learn that love is greater and more rewarding than hate, before she departs from this side of the earth and also to find a relationship with her God.

Another one of the **X** factors that interfered with me having relationship with my **son** was the welfare system. It gave mothers a hand-out rather than a way out, and detached the father from the family. It did not provide them with incentives to want to do better. My son's mom had succumbed to that hand-out mentality. She was conditioned by a vicious cycle and encouraged by her mom to remain in that cycle. It also had an adverse effect on me, as the father and because I owe welfare for her being on welfare. But I was paying taxes; I thought that money helped for programs like that. Well if that is the case I should have benefitted from the subsidized housing, and allowed to see my child. How can you make me pay for something that I don't have the privileges of using? It was like paying for a car and I was not allowed to drive, but someone else is allowed to drive my car? They call that back pay. Well, if that is the case. Give me my back visits, and take back the pain you've caused in my life.

The grandmother had her own agenda, and when she became aware that I was on to her, that's when she created this division. I made a few attempts to try to get the mother of my child to move with me; so that we could raise our baby as a family. Well, if I am still searching to have a relationship with my son, after twenty eight years. You already know who the victor was. I truly believe she loves her daughter, and from her perception of the world this was for the good of her daughter. Did she ever consider what was good for my baby boy? Yeah, dam right that's my baby boy and hell yes I get angry sometimes thinking about how someone else's decision changed the dynamics of an entire family. I wonder was this same treatment inflicted upon my son's mother dad. I asked about her father and her mom told me he was dead. Wow! Am I dead too. I "ain't" never giving up on my mission to tell my son I love him, and to one day tell him that I never abandoned him. I am alive, and I am going to let him know it. I will fight until my last breath in my body.

This is one of the many reasons why men are not in the home raising their babies. Why? Because some mothers will hold onto anger, and that anger leads to resentments, and resentments leads to a calloused heart. Mostly, too because men are not family oriented when they have a child and the children are not planned. These babies are products of us just having sex, and not being conscious of our sexual encounters. In America there are families being born out of wedlock, because they are not couples first. They are sex partners who have children. Once upon a time in our society this type of behavior was shunned upon, and was hidden and shameful to the family. The child would be relocated down south, to be attended to by kin folks.

There has been a shift in morals, and now having a baby out of wedlock is celebrated. The Hollywood industries are capitalizing on the crisis of babies having babies, by making reality shows and glamorizing this illusion on the (tell –a –lie vision) that it is acceptable. I hear women talking like, "girl you coming to my daughter's baby shower, she's having another baby by some guy she met up in the club." Yeah I know, right, I hope this "nigga ain't" like her other baby daddy cause that "nigga ain't" got no job, so he can't even pay no dam child support girl." "I know right, but heard this nigga is a real baller." This is coming from the mothers. This is Real Talk, no joke; I have listened to too many of those types of conversations. In the words of Arsenio Hall, "it makes me say mmmm."

Ladies sex ain't love and love "ain't" sex. Men take heed to this, when you have sex with a woman there is always a possibility of creating a life, and that you must be responsible for that life you've created. **Here is my perspective**: you have to realize that the man is supposed to be the head, but women you are the neck and without the neck the head has nothing to support it, if there's no neck the head cannot function at all. My point here is that a man will do almost anything for sex, so it is vital for the ladies to set the standards on how the sex will be distributed. Ladies don't miss this one, if you conduct yourselves like queens; then you are going to only attract kings or something very close to it. The ball is in your court, so don't miss the foul shot. You have to set the standards for those men who don't have any standards. Women you cannot use your physical attributes alone to get a man, because that relationship will not have any substance. You may get the man with your knock out gorgeous looks, but you won't keep him with looks alone. Don't be a dime piece that's only worth a penny. What about being a master piece that is priceless? Don't be used as eye candy for his ego and his sexual appetite. Now on the other hand, if you are well rounded in all the right places, you will catch a well rounded man. Let me clarify well rounded. I'm not talking about having an apple bottom and boobs that stand up like a twenty year military veteran in the position of attention.

I am talking about mentally, emotionally, culturally, educationally, and financially. That makes a person well rounded, that goes for both genders, and in other words, what you got between your legs is not enough. My brothers, bring something tangible to the table. Like a job, and the ability to complete a sentence. The point here is that both parties need to bring something to the table. This allows the relationship to nourish, and help the relationship to grow and not die from starvation. This nurturing is needed from both parties to keep the relationship healthy.

I believe women should have higher moral standards, because this will encourage men to be responsible for the treatment of their women. They will have to step their game up, and provide more than sweet nothings in a woman's ear. That being said, it was time for me to confront myself and make some mature decisions in my life, because it is no longer about me. Because of those sweet nothings in her ear, a baby boy is here. Michael Jackson's lyrics said, "I'm looking at the man in the mirror, if you want to make the world a better place take a look at yourself and make that change." It was time for me to make that change. You see, I cannot make another person accountable for their actions, but I can be accountable for my actions. And like Spike Lee said, "Do the right thing." The right thing for me was to attempt to confront my son's mother in a civil manner, and propose a plan of action and make an attempt to become a responsible parent for the life we created. The operative word here is **we**, because as this story proceeds "we" would become non-existing. For the sake of their child the parents have to be willing to work on maturing, so that they can obtain the life skills for maintaining a respectful relationship. Those innocent babies deserve nothing less, so that they can have the best opportunity for success. Parents stop! It is time to put your pride and differences aside, and become mature, loving, and nurturing parents. It can be done; if we take the first step. Parents the journey of a thousand miles begins with the first steps. This poem speaks volume to the external and internal factors that can disrupt a child's life. **I wrote a poem about want to hear?**

It Ain't About Me and You

I'll take some of the responsibility for our hopelessness. But some of the blame is on you too, it's not all my fault that your life has been reduced to looking out of the window of what could have been. Now you're mad at every man that crosses your path, because of the choices you made.

It took two to make three and now you're mad at me. Had we known the fifteen minutes of oh baby, ah baby this is the best I ever had, would lead to a life of pain and hate towards one another. Now we hate on each other like two steps brothers born from separate mothers.

We're only focusing on two, and that's me and you. We have fallen into this self-destructive behavior of it's all about me. We need to open up our eyes to see that it ain't about you and me, but the number three. We got to realize our wrongs and make them right, so we both can be at peace when we sleep at night.

Because we hurt each other when we fight and act wild; when we should be thinking of our precious beautiful child. Yeah, I know I said that I'll never leave and that I'll always love you, but it's no longer about me and you. So, what are we going to do?

This poem was inspired because I wanted to see my son, and be a part of what I had produced. I was in a lot of pain, and writing about it helped alleviate that aguish. I wanted to spend time with my son. Was that an unreasonable request? Well, the court system thought it was and my son's mom though it was an unreasonable requests for me to want to spend time with my boy.

The greatest atrocity that parents can inflict on their children is not investing quality time. They have created this delusional world of material things to replace those things that are intangible, which cannot be replaced with things. Parents we have convinced ourselves if we buy our children more things and provide them with all the modern world gadgets that this would make us feel better. This will somehow make up for the time; reality check parents we cannot replace time with things. Material things will not replace the two jobs and make up for all the times when I did not show up for their extracurricular activities. The times I did not show up for their recital, school play, football game, and the countless other events, because I was trying to accomplish more money to buy my kids more things. The things they needed the most I could not give them and that was my time, because my time was spent trying buy them things that would replace me not having time for them. **Does that sound familiar to any parents out there!** I recall vividly the time my daughter brought to my attention that she would rather have her daddy spend time with her than all these things I was buying her.

I would pick my daughter up from her mother house and she would stay with me, and I would give my girl friend money to take my daughter shopping. I would instruct my girl friend to buy her whatever she needed and wanted. She would buy her three or four dresses, three coats, three or four pairs of shoes during these shopping sprees. The point here is even when I would get her from her mother's house; I still was not spending quality time with my daughter. I would buy her and my girl friend some carry out food; let them shop until they drop. I will hit the club about ten on Friday's and Saturdays and even on Sunday's. What time did I spend with her?

Parents, poverty does not make a mother or father a bad parent. It's when we fail to teach them the essential ingredients for their survival. Our children need to be taught morals, values, and hope. Teach them to dream, and tell them where they live does not determine where they can go. Teach them the value of time. My friend the Honorable Judge Mays said, "When you kill time you murder opportunities." I concur one hundred percent with that statement. Ask me how I know? I wasted twenty years being angry, bitter, and blaming others for my actions. The results was drugs, crime, and the production of nothing but negativity. I woke up twenty years later to the realization that I had nothing to represent for the life that God had given me. Parents teach your children to be productive with their time. The problem in the homes is this; The parent can't teach their children if they don't know anything themselves. You can't give what you never had. I know there are no magic formulas or guarantees to having a well rounded productive child, but parents we must make every effort to do better. Maybe the first place to start is with ourselves; we have to change the narrative. The tone in which we address each other can be a starting point. Stop using derogatory language towards each other because it only brings us down and not build us up. Language such as, "she ain't" nothing but a bitch and hoe. A women like buses there's always another one coming, and a women come a dime a dozen. There are many more, but you get the point. Women you can break a man down too with your words of venom, "He ain't shit he cannot keep a job; all he good for is some dick." All men are dogs, and I don't need a man anyhow." "You ain't nothing like the white man, who makes money and know how to take care of business." "What I need a good for nothing man for?" All the while she tearing this man down his son is a witness to this anger and outburst towards his daddy. Men and women we can be upset or even angry at each other, but we got to do it in a respectable and loving way. Just because we don't see eye to eye don't mean we can't see each other, so let us not be blinded by our own lack of vision.

The maturity had arrived and I wanted nothing more than to be a dad, and be responsible like the man my dad is. The poem was trying to reflect the point, that whatever happens between us, it was not about us, it was about the child and as parents we must try to keep that at the forefront, and put our petty differences aside. What can be more important for a man than to raise and nurture his child? I cannot think of anything more important. I had an epiphany and nothing was going to stop me from fatherhood. However, there are things that I describe as the X factors that were beyond my control. One of those **X factors** was two loved deprived women, who could not see beyond their anger. There would be other X factors like a hostile jurisdiction system that only saw me as a pocketbook to feed their deceptions. Man, I could not fathom in a million years the horror that I was going to encounter. My life and my son's life was about to enter into the twilight zone. This emotional roller coaster ride was going to take us on some highs and lows that would cause our ride to be uncomfortable. My son and I are going need extra safety equipment, because seats belts will not be enough to keep us safe from the emotional turbulence that this ride called life would take us on. What I was put through by the manufactured X factors made me questioning my manhood. Did I have anything to give as a parent, as a husband, and as a man?

The choices in my life would dictate my life. I hear this lot in church, if you are not equally yoked, the relationship is doomed to fail, but there was never a relationship in the first place. It was a booty call for me. This encounter was toxic from the very start. The singing group New Edition explained it well. "Never trust a big butt and smile, because she's dangerous." "That girl is poison." I learned the hard way about having sex under the influences of drugs and alcohol, because my inhibitions are weakened when they are under the influences of mind altering substances (Drink). Now twenty eight years later, I am still paying child support for a child I never had a chance to love or be included as a part of his life. I am just another account due on their revenue spread sheet at the Child Support Enforcement Agency.

Whatever she thought we had, it was not a relationship. I did not have a relationship with myself; I was in a self-destructive and self-pity state of mind. Here she was an emotional fragile woman, and what I have discovered about the disease of alcoholism. I was in the early progression of becoming an alcoholic; if I was not already one. Here is the scenario: Two unstable women and an alcoholic man and an innocent child. What we needed doing those turbulent times was counseling and parenting skills, and for all the outside interference removed. What will transpire from the birth of this miracle? Readers let me make a point here if you are going to have a child do the foot work, so that that child can have an opportunity at this thing called life. Do a genetic test, and check to see if there is a history of mental illness/alcoholism. What I am conveying is make an attempt to control those external factors that you can. Children should not have to suffer from the actions of immature and selfish parents. They already got the deck stacked against them prior to being born, especially when the birth is not planned and the parents are not financially and mentally capable of taking care of themselves. Now put all that together and add a pile of vindictiveness to it and those manufactured X factors. It spells chaos and confusion, for the parties involved. First, a relationship should be based on what each individual desires are, and have shared and realistic expectations. Then the two of us should have had a plan of action to coalesce and bring our hopes, dreams, and ideals to fruition. There must be a plan implemented for our lives, and work together to obtain a productive life as best we know how. The problems arise when we skip all the other steps in the developmental stage, and go right into the love phase of the relationship. The love phase is the emotional stuff, the feel-good to me stuff. The passionate, I felt the earth move, type of sex. Only to find out nine months later, after the baby is born that is was not the earth moving; it was the bed sliding on the wooden floors. A reminder women sex "ain't" love, and sometimes men and women are looking for love in all the wrong places. I discovered love couldn't be found inside of a woman's vagina. I did not know how to love another human being, until I learned to love Arnold; now I have something that is transferable to another human soul. Today I can put something positive into the universe, which produces beneficial qualities in others lives. I don't have to take from people lives; only to replace it with pain. My relationships with people today, I can pour into them something that is nourishing to their well being. Unfortunately, In the process of learning to love myself I ruined many women and caused them to lose their own self-worth. I scarred them emotionally. Leaving the baggage for another man to carry, and to try to heal the emotional scars of the pain I created. It will take a strong emotionally stable confident brother to carry that heavy load, and the right women to allow him.

Men why do we need to have more than one sex partner? You know what's fucked up is that we do it over and over again. Now she's damaged goods, because of this sick mentality of men who are emotionally damaged themselves. Damage from low self- esteem and psychological oppression the world has inflicted on their mind. The only relief he thinks available for him is the strong black women, and he willingly and unwillingly abuses her. This Black woman is the only person that will be good to him and is good for him. We don't understand that these strong black women are the greatest asset we have, but we continue to bankrupt them emotionally.

Men, we put babies in them and then want to abandon our role, and make all types of excuses why we cannot be a responsible parent. Some people's situations may be similar to mine, where you were denied the opportunity to be a dad, because the mother had motives that were not the norm. In her irrational state of mind she only wanted to create pain for the father, so she denied her son and me our right to have a relationship. Her only mission in life was to cause pain, and use our son as a pawn in her unrealistic world. Men love your children if you have them in your life. Please! I beg you for me, because I never had that chance. Oh, the many silent tears I have cried, and my son has never heard my cries for him. This book is my cry for help. All I wanted to do is hug my son and tell him I love him; before I take my permanent dirt nap.

The issue of me trying to have a relationship was based completely on the views of Danita's mother. Now I have encountered another one of those X factors, trying to decipher what the grandmother wants. This was the only way I was ever going to have any time with my baby boy, and she made that clear in all our encounters. It was her way or the highway, and she had every move down like a master chess player: From the time I could see him, how long I could see him, where I could see him. Basically, this baby was hers' and she was not letting anyone come between her and my son. She was always looking for innovative ways to get money. Her decisions changed the lives of so many people. The list is too long to name. My point is lives have been forever altered because of this woman's decision making. Arnell only got to see his grandmother on his father's side (T. Momma), maybe a hand-full of times, and one final time at her funeral. She was determined to keep him separated mentally and emotionally from the patriarch side of the family. What kind of person does that?! My son missed out on so many relationships and memories, that could have been authentic, but instead I stare into an emotional and mental photo album of what could have been. When I looked into my photo book and on my walls there are no pictures of him. She's a thief of the worse kind. When a person has something stolen and he /she has insurance at least they can redeem their property lost. How do you get time and stolen memories back? You don't! What do I fill an empty photograph book with?

The point here is I never had an opportunity from the starting gate to infuse my beliefs, and to have a participating role in my son's life. Things would get worse, and I had absolutely no idea what I was in for, because I always consider myself the type of person who could adapt or manipulate my way through life or not feel at all. I had the alcohol to numb my emotional pain in an attempt to take away the fact that I was not able to be a father to my son. See, the world was telling me I did not fit into the framework white America wanted me to fit in. I felt like a square peg trying to fit into a circle, and my efforts to be a man was not sufficient for society. I kept seeing and hearing through the eyes of others perception of me, and I allowed those perceptions to become me. The media was telling poor people like me that

I was lazy, though I worked long hours for low wages, because I was always told if a man did not work he don't eat. **Here's a suggestion: According to the views of the rulers of the money structure in America and abroad have labeled the strong Black man shiftless. This is oxymoron, because the lazy is calling those who have worked tirelessly for centuries to build their wealth, and never received a red cent for their back braking labor. What I can't comprehend is when we were working for free there were no talk of laziness, until we asked for livable wages after slavery, and demanded to be in their unions. They depleted the vibrant jobs in our community and shipped them to the outskirts of the city or out the country. The result of this caused poverty not laziness, and with a school system based on the income of the community. This created a failing schools system. If you are one of the select few to have a job in the New World Order economy, which is designed to keep the worker class " JUST OVER BROKE"(JOB). Therefore, keeping the hard working people in the vicious cycle of poverty and despair. If the X Factors wanted to they could immediately bring jobs back to this country, and cease this attack on the poor. Reader you do know that poverty is a man made creation. This would eliminate poverty and that laziness the power structures are claiming. Real Talk!**

I could not escape their reality no matter how hard I tried to fit into society's norm. I always felt like someone was judging or labeling my efforts. I was told things like: the black man wasn't smart enough, the black man were dogs. Then to have that confirmed by my black woman that I had to do better, and I should learn to be more like the white man. Everything I tried to accomplish was compared to the white man accomplishments. What a blow to my self-esteem. Then I met the Danita's mother, and I discovered that I was out my league, I was no competition for this rancorous woman. Nevertheless, I made numerous attempts to break through the callousness with charm, money, and of course broken promises. Money would be the key to seeing my son, I discovered that early on. I would provide my son's grandmother with twenty five or thirty dollars for her pleasures. That bought me a few precious moments on the clock with my son.

Now maybe I could share my vision of being his dad, but my thinking was too askew during this transformation. I would learn to see the world from different lenses. I now wanted nothing less than to be involved in my son's life, but I hated having to go through a third party, fourth party, and fifth party. I needed more than a fleeting moment with my son. The parties involved were Danita's mother, Child Support, the Legal System, and the Bureau of Motor Vehicles, as well as the many other X factors that hindered me from being a father to my son. Again, I was not a saint either, but my son and I did not deserve such a harsh and cruel punishment. They sent a brother through loopholes that I never knew existed. This struggle of trying to support myself and stay out of jail and focus on gainful employment; was a constant psychological struggle. I felt like I was always carrying buckets of water up a steep hill, and I was not allowed to spill any, if I spill one drop, I would have to start all over again, and eventually I dropped the bucket and said, "Hell with climbing this hill."

The ability to confront and communicate with the lady I shared sex with, and had a baby with would never transpire. The relationship was always strained and rancorous. I made the decision to pursue the same legal system, hoping it would have the same benefits for me that it had for Danita. I borrowed money from my dad to obtain a lawyer, so that I could start the process of getting the money they were taking from my check modified. The child support system was having me pay based on what my previous job income was. I tried to explain to the system that I did not have that job anymore, and that I was unable to pay their ransom that they wanted for my freedom. Now of course, I ain't told those folks downtown that. They show "nuff" would of locked my black ass up. The system told me, "It does not matter, because I had the potential to earn what I was previously earning." Well if this was the case, I had the potential of becoming a billionaire. Man, I tell you it is a struggle trying to get compassion from this money making machine. They make you pay if you want to do this if you want to do that. It will have you pulling your hair out if you got any; hell they took that too, my hair I mean. I had many sleepless nights worrying about keeping a job, my son, and going to jail again. That shit was torture. Under the advice of my lawyer, he told me to pay constantly for a year, and that I would have no problems getting visitation rights. I waited for a year and half, thinking this will give me more leverage in the courts system, and improve my odds of finally being able to assume my natural born inheritance as a father.

Nope, it would not happen. I was told by a court system that I was not granted visitation rights, and they provided no explanation. They were considerate enough to allow me the privileges' to write my son letters. What the fuck I was not in prison. Why do I have to write a letter? My tears fell like rain; I had to pull my hoopdi (car) off the road onto a safe place to gather my thoughts. I was devastated to say the least. It would become a constant uphill battle for me just to try to see my son. It was not mama baby, and daddy's maybe, because I never refused or denied that Arnell was my son. Yes, I am the father of Arnell, and I am not just a check every two weeks. I am a man who loves his son, and a desire to be a father with my imperfections and all. As a father my child is part of me, and naturally I want to love and protect my child. Somehow my desire to love my child has been slandered, and now I have to fight to change the narrative as to why I want to be a father to my child. It has become a battle between the system, and the mother to be included in the narrative of my son's life.

Part of the solution to this conundrum of babies having babies is that our children need to grasp the harsh reality of raising children. Those who are proponents of sex education they need to be willing to expose children to the ugly truth of raising a baby. If not this vicious cycle will continue to be a thorn in the side of our communities. Our children must be taught the rudimental skills of what is required to raise a human being. They need to know that it will take emotional and financial skills, because babies just do not grow up on their own, and you don't get money from a money tree. There are certain things a baby requires so that they can have a chance to endure the rigorous challenges of life growing pains. Hell, it is hard to raise a child with two balanced and sane parents, so imagine a single mother who is financially disabled, unskilled, and has no support systems. Parents it is time to stop turning a blind eye to this crisis, and glamorizing sex. The horrible aspect of this crisis is that children are not seeing enough positive examples of loving committed relationships from their parents or adults in general. If we are going to accept our babies having babies then we (the community) must find means to feed, house, and educate them, so that they can have the best possibilities to maintain themselves as adults. The community must begin to educate our boys on what it takes to be a man. A possible start could be to teach them to first love, respect, and to protect their women. If they don't protect their own, they will never be respected by others, and the black woman will never respect her black man. There has to be someone to project that positive image of a black man, and if the role cannot be played by the biological father then: a church member; the business owner at the corner store; the uncle; a community member. Someone has to take an interest in our babies, I don't want to over use the cliché, but it is going to take a village to raise our babies. Most importantly, we got to stop allowing our children to be raised by their friends and those manufactured X factors like the Hollywood Industry. Turn off those tell a lie visions, and spend some time with them doing something thought provoking. Parents we are and should be their vision and guidance that enables them navigate through the rough waters of life. The entertainment industry sole purpose is to make money and to sell fantasies to our children, and parents are allowing it, as a matter of fact, parents are helping to promote the poison fed to our precious babies.

Parents listen to this point, it's extremely important, we have to find the time to cultivate our children minds, and stop telling them we "ain't" got time. Now that the sex is over, parents our now faced with the challenges of raising a child, which is an ongoing life time investment. Parents what do we have to invest into our children, or better yet what are we willing to invest is our children is a better question? We cannot know someone if we don't spend time with them, because our children live with us, does not mean we know them. Are we spending time to know our precious children? **I wrote a poem about it, want hear it?**

We Ain't Got Time

**We put our childrens name to shame, because
we don't have time for them.
We're too busy seeking social fame and
trying to act like them because,
We ain't got time.
Our precious babies are crying at our feet,
but we sooth them with television,
Rap, B.E.T. and bad T.V. are now making their decisions.
Parents we're acting confused because we
have allowed our children to be used
by this negative media tool.**

Now you got little Ray Ray bragging on how he's pimping his hoe
While hanging out in front of the Arab store.
And Big Mike is talking about killing his own
brother, because he sold crack to their mother.
Look like we ain't ever going to learn to love
one another because we ain't got time.
We don't have time to teach them about their motherland
because we don't understand the importance of
that, but we can find time to buy crack.
Parents on Friday and Saturday everybody is in the club getting
crunk, and waking up the next morning hung over and still drunk.
Parents we should be teaching our girls how to act like a lady and
our boys how to act like a man, so that they can be all that they can
As parents we need to put positive things on our children
minds instead of partying all the time. Lexus asked her
mother to buy her a math book. Mom replied, "I ain't got
time because mommy needs a new designer pocket book."
Now ten years later little Lexus is all grown up,
and she's hooked, and she spends her hard earned
money on designer clothes and pocketbooks.
Parents we ain't got time, to develop our precious children minds.
Now little Ray Ray and Big Mike are both in jail not because
of the system but because, as parents we've failed.
Parents we got time to do everything else, but
when it comes to our precious children
We put their hopes and dreams on a shelf.
We need to give our children praise and glory,
before they end up on the back page of the
obituary as just another story.
Now here we are again standing on street
corners building ghetto shrines when,
We should have been spending quality time.
Parents let's find the time to cultivate our precious
children mind, and stop telling them
We ain't got time.

--The state of mind of some of our modern day parents, and some have apparently forgotten that parenting is a responsibility so let's start acting responsible for our children

I just want people to learn to appreciate the time we have, and stop allowing those precious moments to aimlessly be used without a purpose. There are too many people who have paved the way for us not to understand that your time is owed to others. Time is the most precious present that God has gifted man with. As people we cannot walk on this earth like our time is unlimited, and that our time is ours to waste. People we have to be mindful that once the moments of time have evaporated it's a rap. It is over, no tomorrows to try to get it right, no do over's. What are you going to do with your moment in time?

My problem I had with women, as I see it now, was my inability to effectively convey my **feelings.** I did not know how to communicate outside the bedroom sheets. Here is a pivotal point in my life that caused me to change. My relationships were never based on honesty. Was this learned behavior or was it because I just couldn't commit? I always thought I needed more. I wanted more but more of what? What was I searching for? Why am I unable to return what was freely given to me? I have had women tell me that they can no longer stay in a one sided relationship with me. They have given every ounce of their love. They felt has if I had not reciprocated their love, and it had left them emotionally drained. This one beautiful God-sent woman I was involved with was a gem, a diamond in the rough. She allowed me back into her life after several years apart. I ran into her in college, of all places. She was pursuing a Bachelor Degree in Psychology at the time. I was on my journey of becoming a better person, and we rekindled old feelings. We started dating, and we did the typical things movies and dinner. When we broke up the first time, it was not for cheating; it was from me being emotionally detached. The break up was amicable. Second time around I would be found guilty of cheating on her. **Here's what happened:** After we began to rekindle old feelings, and I had learn how to be a better listener and more attentive to her needs. I had my own place and she had her own place, but I would visit her place. I did invite her over for dinner and a movie once. I was residing on the North side off of Detroit Ave, and she was not familiar with that side of town at all. We were dating and I enjoyed being with her, but she was not the only one. I had another girl that I had met before meeting her. Well, let me be honest here, I was cheating on her from the very start of the relationship. I tried to sever my ties with of the other woman, but she was like super glue. She was clinging to my every move. I tried to do everything in my power to get rid of her, or maybe not, because I was still fucking her and letting her spend the night at my place. Early one morning out of the blue, I was half sleep and butt naked. I had just finished sexing girly up real good. Bang, Bang! There was this loud thunderous knock at my door. My lady jumped up and opened the door. I grabbed my pistol; because I thought maybe my past had caught up with me. I was caught ass out with this other lady. Both women would interrogate me for hours; until day break. They wanted me to make my decision right then and there. Who I loved and who I wanted to be with? I was in a state of shock. This was surreal; two beautiful black women sitting there patiently questioning me, as if I was being cross examined in the court of law. I was expecting a murder scene or at least some boiling grits thrown on my black ass for my doggish ways, and for mistreating these two women. These two women deserved to be respected and loved, and nothing less. They made me choose, and I chose the one who came to my house four o' clock in the morning banging on my dam door. Let me tell you this, I ended up still dating both of them for about two months, then all hell broke loose. My girl that I loved would discover that she was pregnant, so I was with her more often. Sadly, she could not carry the baby full term. That would have been my opportunity to redeem myself, and be a father through birth to adulthood, and instill in my child the opposite qualities that I was not exhibiting in my life.

I told you early I met her in College, and one day in chemistry class. She totally lost it, and went ballistic on me in front of the entire class exposing what I had done to her. She took the mask off me and allowed the world to see this lying cheating son of bitch I was. My females' classmates dissed me from that day forward and the men acted strange toward me too. Guess, the men were thinking how I could I mistreat such a lovely girl so badly or maybe they were thinking why it was me knocking those boots; instead of them. And she was a very nice woman, I admit. I was not looking forward to that class. I wanted that semester and that class to be over with like yesterday, and for a brief moment I thought about dropping out of school. I was reminded of the pain and destruction that I left behind. I was like a hurricane leaving nothing but devastation and ruins for these ladies to rebuild their lives, and there was no Federal Emergency Management Agency (FEMA) relief to assist these women through their human catastrophic experience of hurricane me.

She was fair looking woman who had great qualities and morals. She did not share her bed with many men. This was a true strong black woman of quality and of high standards. She communicated about everything and I mean everything! She was well educated, smart and did not smoke or drink and enjoyed being at home. She was single and had no children. She was financially stable, which most of the women I dated were. Well, with the exception of my son's mother who got trapped into getting hand outs, and was never encouraged to seek an alternative way out. She became a victim of the vicious welfare system like so many other women who were trying to improve their circumstances in life.

This woman as I would discover, after the fact, was dealing with her own demons. The other woman I had a child with is a great mom, but the challenges of raising four girls on her own; robbed her of the opportunities to pursue her life goals. This woman I would marry twenty years later, only to crush her fragile emotional heart into a million shattered pieces. Unlike the Humpy Dumpy fairytale she may never be able to be put back together again. She is and may be damaged beyond repair, because of my inability to reciprocate what was freely given to me. I come to this realization, because I have acquired the skills of being honest and truthful in my relationships today. I am still piercing the hearts and soul, and ruining the essence of their womanhood. I know love is a difficult concept to grasp, and everyone has their angle or spin on what love is. Let's keep it real, Al Green said it best "love will make you do right and do wrong." Love is a powerful deceitful monster, because when you're in love with someone, the person mind is not capable of rationalizing or processing this feeling of love. All the books and seminars will not help, no expert advice going to help a person when there under the influence of love. The person must seek a power greater than them, and hit their knees and pray for strength and discernment. The only defense from love is God. Women you should have standards and self-worth, because once you give up your precious body it is gone and you can't get it back ladies. If you are going to let a man have it; give it to a man that is worthy of that prized possession. Unfortunately, that may not be good enough because you may come across a master manipulator like me. The problem I have noticed is sometimes an individual man or woman can't identify something good if they have never had it, or what they deem as good. This is why they continue this vicious cycle of choosing people who may not be good for them. Women you can be manipulative too in a relationship, because of the past pain and hurt caused by men. Women you are forward thinking people, and you visualize and plan months and sometimes years ahead from the first encounter of meeting a man. Heck, you've already picked out the wedding dress and a name for the baby on the first hello.

CHAPTER 4

Who Really Benefits?

When I emerged from the fog, things had spiraled out of control. I had lost my driving privileges on several occasions and I could not keep a stable job, and I was denied visitation rights. Times were rough, but I knew this was not going to be my destiny because I knew that the God of my understanding was not going to put on me more than I could not bear. I also knew that my journey was not my destination, and if I just held on to the little bit of hope I had left there would be something greater on the other side. I just had to make it to the other side, so that meant going through to get to the other side.

This was during the Clinton's Administration when they were promoting this Welfare Reform Bill, and the Three Strikes Bill was also on the table. To counter getting mothers off welfare they attacked the dads, and popularized this new term called "**dead beat dad.**" Dads became the focal point of these new laws that were designed to increase the prison population, and transform the welfare system off the backs of the dead broke dads. They made dads totally responsible for a system that was never beneficial to the well being of the family dynamics. The entire welfare system was never designed to be a way out for single mothers, it was more like a handout and it was formulated to alienate the father and disenfranchise him from his family. **Real Talk!**

There should be some shared responsibility with this title of "deadbeat dad." The mothers that do not attempt to get off the welfare program, and those who are able to work and/or attend school, but choose not to attempt to improve their economic status. Women who deprive men the right to raise their children are detrimental to the family dynamics. I am officially titling all mothers who deny fathers of their natural God given right to be a parent, and to be a participant in their child's life as "deadbeat moms." To meet those qualifications for a "dead beat" mom you must deny the father visitation rights and you must be on welfare and not make any attempts to make economic improvements in your life. Oh, sorry I failed to mention they must also be vindictive and bitter. The person, race and economic background excluded.

Psychologically it was a strategic move by the creators of these systematic social economic injustices. They implemented the Welfare Reform Act in 1997, these law makers introduced these arcane laws to create and destroy the structure of families. This was done under the disguise of laws. I coined the phrase "Laws", which means this "W" can be interchangeable. L= **legal**, A= **advancement**, W= **wealthy/white** and the S= **society**. The dual meaning for the" W" is White. These aggressive laws are one of those manufactured **X** factors I mentioned.

I appeared in court in 2001, at another failed attempt to get visitation rights. I was not making progress so I tried to compromise and ask if one of my family members could pick him up, but the mother and grandmother were opposed to any interaction from my side of the family. It was a control factor with her mom, and it became more and more apparent to me that the grandmother control ever facets of her daughter's life. The grandmother would not allow my mother or father to have any interaction or have an active role in my son's life. I really think that did something to my mom more than my dad, because dad did not let much concern him. Well, at least on the outward appearance. My dad reminds me of the Serenity Prayer: "God grant me the serenity to accept the things that I cannot change, and the courage to change the things that I can and the wisdom to know the difference."

The grandmother would allow me to see my son sometimes for an hour or two, but the mother had to accompany me. This access was only granted when I provided her mom with the financial means to engage in her extracurricular activities. It was very frustrating getting arrested for child support, and trying to cough up money I did not have. I was losing my license every other month, and had to pay reinstatement fees to the Bureau of Motor Vehicles (BMV) on each occasion. I could not maintain a stable job, because I was unable to get to where the jobs were. It was a difficult time in my life, because I didn't see a solution in sight to this nightmare. I often wished that it was in a dream, and I would wake up and the nightmare would vanish. Well, regrettably I never woke up because the nightmare continues. The well paying jobs were usually not on the bus routes, and if they were on the bus line, the buses were not running when I got off of work. I remember working as a dishwasher, and prep cook, and how difficult it was to keep that job because I did not have license or reliable transportation to get to work. I caught that last bus to work, and most of the times I could hustle a ride to the bus stop. My reliable ride quit his job, and I was forced many nights to walk late at night from Red Lobster to the bus stop to catch the number 4 bus on Chagrin. This was about a five to six mile walk; it seemed that long. I know realistically it had to be three miles. To make matters worse, try adding the Detroit's winter into the equations. I tried desperately to hold on to that job, because I actually loved learning to cook and being in the restaurant business. No matter how much I loved that job, it would become too much to bear.

I was forced to quit because I just could not endure the strenuous walk every night. There were other incidences where transportation impeded my employment. It is like I am constantly dodging daggers, no matter how hard I try not to get hit, there were just too many daggers coming too fast at one time. I'm not trying to make excuses for not always paying child support, but my life and my finances were unstable. Yes, I should have been financial stable, no doubt, and I don't, and will not refute that point. I just knew there had to be a better way to get back on my feet and stay there, but how the system is designed it is not set up that way for me to get up and stay up. I will say that they should not have locked me up in jail, a day after burying my mom. Those things left a bitter taste in my mouth for my son's mother and the manufactured X factors which happen to be the powerful and ruthless Child Support Enforcement Agency (CSEA). To add insult to injury the jailers lost my mom's favorite hat that I was wearing. Danita could have explained my circumstances and asked for them to postpone my jail date. That type of mindset is compatible only to the deeds of our current political leaders in America. She displayed no compassion for me, and that same behavior was on display at my mom's going home service.

I was trying to stay gainfully employed, and be available for my mom during her illness. I was one of the members in the family responsible for driving my mom to and from dialysis. Yes, I drove under suspension, but that's my mother and I didn't give a fuck about their unfair money making laws. I was going to do what I had to do to help prolong her life. This was not fair to my mother. My licenses were suspended under the new Welfare Reform Act, which allows child support to take your driving privileges, not because I had violated the driving laws of the state. This is one of those manufactured X factors that creates unnecessary anxiety in your life. It was a tight rope act for me to maintain my core sanity, and if you factor in the X factors: denied the right to see my child, constant unstable employment, poverty, living in crime infested war zones, police brutality, and an ailing mom. Those were some trying times; had it not been for a mighty God I serve. Well, maybe a mighty God who is favoring me with his mercy. I had to find an outlet that was more productive than drinking and drugging. I discovered writing poetry when I was child, and it had a tremendous therapeutic value for me then. I would begin to beckon that inner voice, which would bring me inner peace, and eventually help to save me from me. This poetry was my spiritual awakening, and I begin to have a since of power in my life. I decided to be strong and not to continue to allow those manufactured X factors to dominant my life. I will use my inner voice to sooth the anger, pain and the hurt inside of this lost man child who seeks peace from being a broken dad.

I began to organize and speak out, and get involved in my neighborhood and with the political machine. I knew I could no longer allow things that I could not control have control over me. That included: Danita's mom, Danita, my alcoholism, hopelessness, and a defeated attitude. I was no longer going to hold my head down, and feel like I did not deserve to breathe the same air that God gave all humans to breathe. I took a deep breath and was going to take this life God gave me, and become the best person I knew how to be. Maybe if I gave it a try, I could live life to its full potential? I could show my son that I was not this horrible monster those manufactured X factors had painted me to be. I was determined to recreate those negative images that the world was depicting of this black man. I took my paint brush and painted my own picture. I am going to write the ending to my story, and was not going to continue to allow others or any of those manufactured X factors to be the publisher of my life. I edited negative things and influences out of my life.

I was really dealing with some serious challenges, being denied my parental rights to my child. This was psychologically damaging, and the pain took me to places where I should have never gone. For a long time, I could not come to face the reality of the ideal of not being allowed to be in my son's life. I know now that self annihilation was not a logical choice. This pain provided me the excuses to justify making those self-destructive choices. The decisions I made dictated my life. What I have learned in this growing process from a boy to maturing into a man of character. Was this, whatever decision I make bad or good, I must be responsible and move forward building upon those experiences. I must make each yesterday, each step and everyday better than the previous moments. I must make my foot prints impressionable enough, so that others may be inspired to fulfill their destinies in life.

I would like my legacy to be that each day I made those around me light shine a little brighter. I also want the world to know that I never stop fighter for my natural God given right to be a father to my son, and to tell my son that I love him with every being of my soul. If God see fit to never allow my son and I to see eye to eye maybe this book will get to him, and if it does; son spoken out of the mouth of your dad, I love you with every **breathe that I have been allowed to take on God's green earth.**

Here is one of the many letters I have written to you son over the years:

Hello, Ms. Danita and Mr. Arnell. I sincerely hope that these words have meaning, and that this letter finds the family in good health, mentally, and spiritually. I write to say that I continuously pray that God keep you guys in his safe haven. I also pray that God will shed the light of hope and peace in our lives, so we will know his will for us and not function on our will. That we can one day sit at the table of love and kindness and not carry that heavy load of disdain and discord towards one another.

I would not be honest if I told you that I was not dishearten and sadden over the years for not having an opportunity to play my natural role as a loving and caring father, which is essential in the development of

a child. However, I place the blame on no one's shoulders but on the shoulders where the blame belongs.

Most importantly, I pray that there will come a time in the near future that we will all share in that peace and joy only God can provide, and be able to transfer that love to one another. I still retain in my heart the hope that one day this will come to fruition.

I am also saddened by the fact that two consenting adults made a self-serving decision to cater to their own personal agenda. Denying a deserving child his once in a life time opportunity to know that feeling of unconditional love from two wonderful and caring parents. I pray that before the gate of death consumes us we will make things right by God and Arnell. I know that my God can soften a callous heart, and unveil the compassion and love that lies beneath that surface of hate.

Never the less, I do understand that your agenda has not altered, and I will do everything in my human power to pay the juridical system their money, and hopefully that provides the satisfaction you have been seeking. I realize that there will be no cordial dialogue until these monetary issues are resolved.

"Let Us Pray in our hearts that God make away for Us"

Arnell if you get this letter I would say to you, "Love is the greatness character of a man, and to always pursue your dreams." Never allow anyone to deny you of hope, and always look beyond the surface. Lastly, but not least always think for yourself. If you adhere to these suggestions you will be just fine. Hope to see you soon and I miss you. Arnell I miss you and I will always carry the wounded scars of love in my heart for you. I am always accessible and available to you, because I Love You!

This letter is one of many I have written over the years to try to erase the pain in my heart, and to stop these tears.

I wrote this letter 9/12.

The results were the same I never got a response. I will keep fighting for the right to tell my son I never abandoned him, and that I will always love him, and despite the wall of resistance I will not stop. My son deserves to know that I love him.

Who benefits from me not being in my son's life? The manufactured X factors are the only one benefitting from my involuntary exclusion from my son's life. I tell you who benefitted and there's a healthy list and enough deception to go around. **Who Benefitted?** The Feminist Movement definitely had a devastating impact in helping to create this vacuum of fatherless homes. How? We know the unemployment of Black youths and the Black male adults are nearly doubled and in some place triple of that of the White population. That means the already limited job opportunities for the Black man would now be divided amongst the white women and black women. This Feminist Movement increased the women opportunities for gainful employment and decreased the already limited gainful employment for the black males. The Feminist Movement moved the black male right out of the job market and right out of the homes. It created a man against the woman environment; thus, creating more separation and division amongst the family. Now there are women wanting to be equal to the men. Make no mistake here; I want women to be independent and to be able to flourish, and to have their own ideals and businesses. I guess what I am trying to understand is, if women are to be equal, how do we distinguish the difference between the role of the man and the role of the woman. Is that not against the natural order of nature? I don't know, it's something to ponder.

One of the devices used in their plot to annihilate the family is to divide the family by implementing the Welfare System as we know it today. The initial purpose was to give a person a way out of their penniless situation, and provide temporary assistance until the economy improved. They created a program called Work Relief because so many people were jobless. This system was originally intended for white farmers to supplement them during the turbulent times after the 1929, stock market crash resulting in what was called the Great Depression during this time.

This was part of President Roosevelt's New Deal Act, to help the suffering people. The difference in white and black's receiving welfare was the purpose behind it, when whites got welfare it was a temporary way out, but for blacks it was a hand out; rather than a way out of despair. It paralyzed the black man and his family.

African Americans have always doubled the unemployment of white Americans. What's being done for the black male who is unemployed and needs a job? Are the manufactured X factors declaring a crisis and forming a job bill act? No they are creating jobs off the backs of blacks through the prison system. To further clarify what has happen to the disenfranchised here are two letters written by the author:

Fatherless Father

The current child support law appears to be a replica of the Black Code Laws. These laws were implemented in 1865, after the Civil War for the purpose of denying former slaves the opportunity to obtain financial freedom. In many states, if unemployed, blacks faced imprisonment. Apparently child support has taken a page out of history, because they can now take a man's license and lock him away in jail because he is unable to pay a debt, and after serving time, this debt is not alleviated. Men are unjustly locked up not because they are unwilling to pay, but because they do not have the means to pay. This is where the distinction of being a "dead beat" dad and "dead broke" dad. Minorities and poor whites are unfairly targeted by this legalized extortion. There is an urgent need for a resolution to this critical issue, so that fathers can resume their roles as fathers and maintain the family structure as financial and emotional providers.

Father's role is to provide for his child emotional and financial. However, there can be obstacles beyond his control. For example, the government never implemented any programs for the indigent fathers into the family structure. The real concerns have never been addressed. Such needs as; being unskilled and undereducated in a school system that prepares poor children for prisons and not corporate America

This results in a myriad of people demanding that poor people get jobs, and join mainstream society. However, unlike President Roosevelt

during the Great Depression, he had a plan; those plans excluded African Americans because of the nature of their employment which was domestic and agriculture. Today's welfare plan unfortunately, does nothing to enhance the economically disadvantaged. Furthermore, these institutions continue to perpetuate this pernicious cycle that have demoralized the poor by legally taking money from those who least can afford it. Here is an overview of the current welfare plan:

- Back child support
- Non-custodial parent assumes all the economic responsibility for the custodial parent being on welfare
- Provide minimum wage jobs/ no medical coverage
- Separation of family/creating Parent Alienation Syndrome
- Shift total responsibility for poverty to the father

Welfare falsely projected an image that the system was designed for the purpose of uplifting poor families. Nevertheless, in their deception, they have allowed generations of families to rely on handouts rather than a way out. Welfare narcissist view claims that it was the indigent fathers fault for not lifting his family from the depths of poverty. These institutions created this system to control and deceive a certain group of people. Welfare never offered or provided viable training prior to the 1997, Reform Act. This flawed system continues to mislead the public of their real intentions by using smoke and mirrors to solve complex, but simple problems. This issue must be addressed. This is like trying to stop a bullet wound from bleeding with a band aid. These poor families do not need more social pacifying programs. They need solutions instead of jails and institutions. These fathers need an economic plan so they can take care of their families like God planned. Amendments are urgently needed to alleviate this family crisis, because this current system does not promote family; it promotes incarceration and disunity. This unjust system has distorted, twisted, deceived, and manipulated the public into believing that poor fathers have shunned responsibility for their children. Furthermore, overlooking governmental policies relating to the poor, that affects fathers' ability to be an effective parent.

Here are some suggestions that will alleviate this crisis and bring structure back into families:

- Give indigent fathers an alternative to jail/community service
- Make it mandatory that indigent fathers and the non-indigent fathers participate in the father initiative programs that are offered in the churches and grassroots organizations.
- Offer both parents emotional support, so they can have a functioning relationship; if conditions allow
- Make it legal for the indigent fathers to claim their children on their tax return; if the mothers are receiving welfare benefits
- Amend hostile laws imposed on the indigent father: Taking their license; Eliminate potential earning clause law which makes it impossible to receive a modification, the current law states that a person has the potential to earn what loss or no income; then the person volunteers to go to jail

Amending these unjust laws will alleviate this legalized extortion called; "back pay" support, and help these poor fathers decrease this insurmountable debt. This would motivate welfare recipients to get off welfare. It is ironic that this law is called back pay; when African descendants requested their "back pay" for working for free, there was an outrage in this great country.

Finally, the system needs to enact a just system that reinforces the family structure and one that is less hostile towards the indigent fathers. The most important part of this equation is our children. They are being used by this bureaucratic shuffle, and left to swim upstream without a life jacket. Justice for the indigent fathers will come through unity and from the resonating of their voices to the masses for justices. It is apparent that our "politrickians" lack humanity, and are unwilling to jeopardize their political careers for these indigent fathers/families. Fathers hear this cry, we can no longer watch on the sidelines and complain; nor continue to accept the role of victims. Now is the time to display to our children that we are not spineless cowards, and we will fight for our natural God given rights to be fathers to our children. Despite the inconceivable obstacles ahead, we must stop this legal but illegal business of profiting off of the pain and suffering of our families. We must not allow them to continue to dismantle the institution of our families.

A Fathers Cry

Second letter:

The Fathers Cry

Specifically, how does it benefit the children if the Child Support Enforcement Agency (CSEA) is imprisoning and revoking poor fathers' licenses because of their inept employment and economic deficiencies? How can fathers become the back bones and the heads of their house hold if CSEA's current laws are allowed to exist? Legally and morally, fathers should have an opportunity to nurture, cultivate, and support their children. Apparently, America's ideology of lifting oneself up by their boot straps has not trickled down to the poor working fathers in America; thus, making it more difficult for them to achieve economic success when their boots and their straps have been taken away. According to the 2000 census data, Cleveland State University researchers informed the Urban League that 345 of Cleveland's 242,481 African Americans live in poverty and about 46% of employable blacks are without jobs (Plain Dealer Dec 8, 2003). Fathers must unite and lift their voices to demand that CSEA offer something other than jail. They must demand gainful employment, psychological support, and that these current laws are amended.

Fathers pride themselves in being gainfully employed and taking care of their families. However, when money from gainful employment ceases to exist then that pride can dissipate rapidly. The lives of these poor fathers begin to regress and they find themselves in a crisis. In addition to their misfortune, they are confronted with the assassination of their character by being labeled "dead beat" dads when in fact, they are "dead broke "dads. There is an obvious distinction between the two.

Furthermore, it appears that CSEA's primary role is not to promote the welfare of the family because if it was why not attempt to uplift these poor fathers so they can have a positive impact. Every statistic and data has supported the significant impact of having the fathers in their children's lives. Dr. Frances Cress Welsing, a psychologist and author of *The Isis Paper* states, "Denial of full scale employment results in the demise of the Black males because they are unable to adequately support themselves, their wives and their children" (V). The results are that a number of Black male children grow up without their fathers' guidance. This leads to frustration, depression, and failure in school.

Millions of children are fighting a courageous battle growing up in working poor families where fathers are playing by the rules, however, cannot earn livable wages or receive adequate support from their government that will allow them to better themselves (Covenant xiv). Who will hear the silent cries of these fathers who want to escape from poverty but just do not have the resources. This constant uphill battle takes its toll on them psychologically and becomes too much for them to bear.

Psychologically, these fathers can become emotionally distraught when opportunities continue to evade them. Imagine the mental anguish these poor fathers endure by not being able to establish a loving and nurturing relationship with their children. Equally important, who authorized CSEA the right to constitute the role that these fathers can play in their children lives based solely on income?

Children need psychological support from their fathers. Everything is not measured by dollars and cents. For instance, there are things such as producing life, teaching a child how to walk, ride a bike, tucking a child in bed and confirming there's no monster under the bed. Most importantly, just being there to tell them that daddy "loves them" has an impact. These moments are invaluable in any child's life.

Psychologically it would be more beneficial for the family structure if CSEA took a less hostile approach and promoted marriage. Marriage would give the family stability. Specifically, finances would stabilize by having two parents earning an income. Secondly, the statistics for out of wedlock children would decrease drastically. The psychological benefits of having two parents in the home are immeasurable. This also eliminates the single mothers' syndrome, and this is why there is an urgency for amending these unfair laws.

Child Support Enforcement Agency laws need amending to restore the institution of family. Here is a list of a few of the current laws that are not conducive to the family unity:

1) Revoking the indigent father's right to drive
2) Non-custodial parents assume financial responsibility for custodial parent being on welfare
3) Separation of family
4) Fathers jailed for lack of earnings

Here are some suggestions that can alleviate this family crisis:

1) Allow fathers to drive if they are seeking gainful employment; have jobs/ attending school/ medical emergencies
2) Make it legal for indigent fathers to claim their children on their tax returns if the mothers are receiving welfare
3) Offer both parents psychological support so that they can have a functioning relationship, if conditions allow
4) Give fathers an alternative to jail/ community service

Fathers are not requesting these amendments for the purpose of shunning their fatherly responsibilities, but because they want to be responsible fathers. Furthermore, who really benefits from the imprisonment and the revoking of poor fathers driving rights? Certainly the children have not benefitted. These poor father's desperately need these laws amended because current laws do not promote family; they promote incarceration and disunity.

Finally, fathers must not succumb to this child support institution that continues to deny them their civil liberties because of their economic conditions. Poor fathers have endured this continuous psychological attack from this new form of institutional slavery disguised as justice.

Stop locking them up because of their conditions, but give them a fair chance to overcome their conditions. Child Support Enforcement Agency cannot continue to be that Iron Gate to prison, but be that gate to opportunity. Fathers must lift their voices and demand that CSEA offer gainful employment, psychological support, and that they amend these bias laws. They must demand to be fathers' to their children and not allow these bogus laws to be a distraction. This is the fathers cry for support from leaders, community activists, churches, and anyone who wants to save our future generation from this bias system that is designed to keep fathers from being the head of the households. These laws are destroying the infrastructure of poor families and keeping fathers from their natural roles.

Wanted:

People who believe in justice for all, and believe our children deserve a chance.

The business of prisons and the unequal representation are publically trading our children on the stock market, and they are making astronomic profits. My situation alone they have benefitted off the economic disadvantaged to sustain their interest, and as you can see; it not about our children but about their financial agenda. I am going to explain this section very carefully, because I want to illuminate this point to my people as to the game they are running on us, and how by keeping the male and female in the protagonist and antagonist roles. The powers to be are diverting our focus on trivial issues to create division amongst the two. The effects of their X factors creates the idea that we hate one another, but because of the deception parents cannot see that the oppressor is oppressing us both and it is the X factor who are determining the outcome of our lives. In other words, they are pulling the strings and we are but puppets in the scheme of their stage play. How is that? On the stock market commodities are traded. What is commodity? Commodities are goods that can be sold and traded on the open stock market. Well, what that got to do with young black boys and girls?

Business of prison and unequal representation in the criminal injustice system; are designed to fuel this billion dollar industry. Therefore, laws are created to fuel their business to yield a return for the investors of these prisons. This equates to young poor black men going to jail, and getting murked (murdered) by policemen in these Police States they live in. If you took the profit out of the prison system you will see a decrease in the prison population? (Explain). Okay, buckle up tight and put on your thinking cap. I'm about to spit some knowledge and attempt to bring light to darkness. You know that light and darkness cannot share the same space. The light will over power the darkness. What I am going to need from you all is to open your lenses to the world a little wider and for those of you who know about the third eye, I need you to open it as wide as possible. The picture can only be painted if the strokes of the brush are lucid and defined, and the contrast is clear and the medium used is appropriate for the artist. I don't want this to be just words on paper, I want the reader to walk away with a since of desperation and hope; then take the action needed. One man: one woman, one child, one family, one community, one church, one school, and one prayer at a time. This will bring about a change. It is like the wise proverb says how do you eat an elephant? You eat it one bite at a time. I think we can take one community as a model and put all the resources into it. Do like they did in Oklahoma? Sorry, for those who do not know about Black Wall Street?

I will provide a glimpse of Black Wall Street/Little Africa only, because I want those who are not familiar with this information to research it, and share it with your children and family. I want you to use this as a teachable moment. In 1921, Tulsa Oklahoma there was this place where Black African American Negros was extremely successful, and everything in their town was owned by them. I know by today's standards it sounds unbelievable; like a fairytale or a movie. The Black business owners would even loan money to the white people in town. Out of the blue you know how they do? There was an accusation that a Black man did something to a white woman so they burned the Greenwood section of the city down, and the good law abiding KKK citizens killed over three hundred black men and destroyed an estimated 1500 homes and businesses. The sinister tragedy about this domestic terrorism was that they were not allowed to rebuild, and all the original documents of this event was destroyed by the terrorist. Americans be careful when we judge what some deem terrorist acts before examining our history, and just because it happen in the past does not mean it didn't happen. Did you know most terrorism act stems from fear or a feeling of disenfranchisement?

My people what is it for a man to gain the world but lose his soul? We are working more: doing more: consuming and buying more; but getting less and becoming loveless people. I am going to enlighten who the benefactors of this cancerous, diseased, zombie walking state of mind that black men are in. Someone once said, Fifty years from now, it will not matter what kind of car you drive, what kind of house you live in how much money you got in your bank account, or what your clothes look like. But will the world be a better place, because you were important in the life of a child. It is time to take a serious look at ourselves as an individual and as a people, and then get busy doing God's work of restoring and rebuilding of a great nation of people.

CHAPTER 5
Raising a Child

Starting off with a statement that it takes love to raise a child will probably ignite some controversy among those child support proponents. I advocate that love is the most powerful tool for nurturing and cultivating a child's mind. This is the catalysts that will infiltrate to the other areas that require emotional maturation of our human development. Why love instead of money? In a realistic world and rational thinking human being, they know that certain essential and basic needs like food and shelter requires monetary support to establish an environment that will produce love. I support love and believe it should be a priority over money. Think about the moments in your life that you can remember; did it have anything to do with money? The point I am making here is when a man loves his child, and is privileged to be involved in raising that child; those basic needs of food and shelter will be an involuntary and uncontrollable reaction. That is the reason I stated love over money. You would not have to tell a human being who is freezing in the winter to put on warm clothes if he has them available to him. You would not have to tell a man to do what's right if love is in his heart. How does a father not take care of his precious miracle from God? How does a society that claims to be founded on the beliefs of a loving God not want to establish laws that encourage marriage and two parent households? In which, the father and mother has an established role, and the two complement each other. I wanted to be that person to establish my son's morals and values so he would be a well rounded person. Although I **did not** have the honor of raising my boy; my younger brother raised both his boys. So I would like to take a moment to acknowledge my brother, and tell him that I admire and envy the fact that he was a father to his children. He was not without blemishes or flaws but he hung in there, and made a positive influence in his boy's lives. During the time I was writer this book my brother and lovely sister- law have been married for twenty three years, and have been together for twenty –eight years. They endured the storms and fought through the challenges; unlike myself. I ran at the slightest thing that made me uncomfortable. Bro you're a chip off the old block. I admire you and Tonya. Thank you for dispelling the stereotypes of the **black father and husband**. Dad and my brother they exemplify the meaning of good men with family values. I know I have the same characteristics, but I think I just was too selfish to relinquish all of me to another human being or maybe I just didn't know how. I guess in a way, I am still that afraid little boy who is scared to face his fears. I can see the benefits it has had on Man and T.J; by my brother and his wife staying together and working things out. Men if we expect our children to change and be responsible, then we must lead the way, because our children need to know morals, values, and hope. Parents teach them to dream, and tell them where they live do not determine where they can go. Teach them the value of time. My friend Anita said, "When you kill time you murder opportunities." I certainly agree with her, because I spent a tremendous amount time doing counterproductive activities. I wasted twenty years of producing negative energy, which led to crime and drugs. When I woke up I realized I had twenty years of nothing to represent the time that God allowed me on this earth. Parents teach your children to be productive with their time. In other word, parents turn off those gadgets for a few hours, and allow their brain to create, and please take those (tell- a- lie- vision) out of their rooms. More importantly, allowing both parents to have a parenting role. This will optimize the opportunity for God's precious miracles to be raised by two parents who loves them. The non-custodial parent should not have to take a back seat to loving their children. That's their God given right to be included; he was included in the bedroom. As the non-custodial parent, I have been in a hostile position since the birth of my son. I feel like I never existed, and my love for my son has no value other than the garnishment of my wages every two weeks.

All I want is to establish a role in my son's life. In my case, I was just trying to establish a chance to see my child without the strong arm tactics of others influence. I applaud those women who have allowed fathers the opportunity to assume their God given rights as fathers, and yet those fathers shun their responsibility. I feel a deep resentment against those men. Here I am fighting for a chance to see my son and to tell him I love him, and then you have some fathers that won't give their children the time of day. I have a strong distaste for those ungrateful selfish assholes! Tears spiral down again, because the thought of any man relinquishing such a privilege and honor of fatherhood; it is hard for me to understand. It infuriates the very core of my humanity, but in the same token my heart has absolutely no empathy or sympathy for heartless mothers who deny men like me their opportunity to be fathers. This is not about pointing fingers and blaming one another, but about adults taking responsibility for a life that both parents created. It does not matter how the baby was conceived into this world; it's about how the baby is received in this world. I have a problem with fathers who are allowed to assume their rightful position, but they refuse to step up to the plate. They don't even make an effort to swing at the ball. They are too sorry to even get in the batter's box and swing; even if they strike out. You made some type of effort! The greatest miracle God has performed is the gift of life. If men are going to have babies, then let's take care of God's precious gifts. Men we have to do a better job, because the relationship with the mother may be hostile, but it does not give us the right to act like children and shun our responsibility as men. We can't under any circumstances allow these mothers to take on the burdens of raising a boy by herself or any child for that matter, it just too hard to raise children today without the help of the father. Men it takes two to have a baby since the last time I heard; even with this artificial reproduction somebody has to produce that sperm that travels into fallopian tube. Men abandon babies grow up to be wounded casualties of war, and if not properly treated it is a matter of time before they explode, because of the unwarranted pain cause by dog ass men. Men we got to stop expecting our children to fight this battle alone, as fathers and as men we have to fight for their lives. We have to stop this professional storytelling, and making these eloquent speeches with empty solutions. Men it is a war on our children, and we can't lie down on the battle field. We can't surrender the white flag to the enemy of fear.

Real Talk Real Men: Men it doesn't make you a real man by having more than one woman, and not cherishing and loving that one woman. No, it makes you a selfish, irresponsible, scared to commit, heart breaking punk bitch! So stop calling yourself a real man if you're still trying to be a player, because no one wins by you being a player. Men acting like boys, and claiming to be men, but what you are really doing is ruining these women lives? Men we must change this irrational thinking, and be the men that God called us to be, and the men that we are more than capable of being. Come on strong black men and stand up! **Here's a question to the men out there. Would you want a man to mistreat your daughters? The answer for me is no; so why would you mistreat and dog someone else's daughter?**

While writing this book, I had to take several breaks because it was emotionally difficult. Those catharsis moments were more than I had anticipated. I needed some comforting, so I called my daughters over and my grandbabies for a movie night. I ordered pizza and picked one of my grandsons up from daycare. I watched my family from afar doing the movie, and I began to appreciate how blessed I am. They were running all over the place getting pizza everywhere, and I had to keep telling them to sit down and stop wrestling with Tyson the two year old. Boy, sometimes those little rascals get on my old nerves. In the totality of it all, I would not exchange those Kodak moments for anything in the world. I love my family with ever fabric of my soul. While savoring in the moment, I felt a sudden sadness again. I thought about how many moments have my son shared with a family who gave him an abundance of love that I was blessed to be a part of. From my twenty eight years of trying to connect with my son, I just cannot fathom him having many loving moment, because of the psychological state of mind of the two women that raised him. How they denied me and my son our God given rights. This innocent child had no say about who his parents were going to be upon his arrival on this earth. Through the grandmother eyes, I was going to take her power of control away. Her agenda to control her daughter and a grandson would abruptly end, because a man was in the picture; that man is the father. The greatest harm in the scheme of things was this grandma took their ability to enjoy life. The real travesty here is this grandmother stole their ability to know any form of love and to think for themselves. What kind of existence can that be? Never knowing the feeling of love or having a relationship with love. I feel so sorry for my son's mom having to be burden with hatefulness; that has to be a living hell. She was robbed of her ability to view the world from a loving perspective. Her mom took advantage of two fragile minds that would never know a world beyond the prison walls that grandma built. Grandmother's agenda was not going to be impeded by some man who wanted to be a father to his son, and take away her daughter and grandson.

I am still trying to understand the grandmother's motives for keeping me out that boy's life. She may have been suffering from her own pain, and that is why she was capable of robbing my son of his birth right, and subjecting an innocent child to this type undeserved stress. She had no moral conviction concerning my son's suffering. I understand the ideal of wanting to punish me for whatever reason, but to punish that baby is baffling to say the least. That included destroying the very thing that she created, a daughter that was reliant on the words of her mother. As the years went by the behavior never deviated, I began to see the pattern in this family. I no longer hold any resentment for them. My anger turned into pity, and I began to pray to God to intervene, so my son could be removed from the grips of bitterness, angry, and hopelessness. I asked God to let me use his eyes to see, so I could understand why this was happening. I remained optimistic because I believed if God could transform my life into the man that he's making me into; then God will surely break the curse of hate. **Mental illness** is not a topic discussed openly in our families. In the chapter on mental illness, I will try to shed some light on this issue, and show how prevalent it is in our communities.

Not being able to be a father to my son made me realize how blessed I was to have a father. **Thanks Dad: Here is a speech I wrote on July 4, 2014 to my father to express my love and appreciation for a job well done in raising a boy into a man.**

Dad I want to apologize for being opinionated, and hollering out I am grown. When in reality I had no clue on how to make it on my own. You allowed me to make my missteps and stumbles, but through it all you never allowed me to fall.

During that time of my maturation I did not understand the process of becoming a man. Thanks dad for showing me that the definition of a man was not measured by the tool in my pants. I learned that a real man did not think below his waist, but above his shoulder.

Thanks dad for the plethora of memories you allowed me to store

Dad I remember you taking the neighborhood kids to Dairy Queen to get a ten cent ice cream in the back of your red pickup truck. You had the red rubber hose on the gear shifter. I remember the time you rented that camper when we stayed on Iowa, and took everybody out of town; I remember when you took us to the race track to see white people drive really fast, and I remember going horseback riding. Today because of the seed you planted, my wife and I want to acquire some land and get some horses donated to create a therapeutic environment for inner city children. That's want real men do, they plant seeds and cultivate them so that they can grow. You don't plant them and walk away from them.

Thanks Dad for having class, because the memories you've created will always last. You see memories will never die, because what you gave me I will with every breath that I breathe pass it to my seeds and cultivate them; so they too may grow.

Thanks Dad for teaching me respect, because that is one thing that will never grow old. You see that thing called respect. You know that song Aretha Franklin sang about; that thing called respect. {As an educator I must uplift and breathe life into my people} Maya Angelou said, "When you get you give, and when you learn you teach." {Women if you don't give it away then the man have to earn it; so stop giving it away. Women do you know; the power that is in your possession? Do you know you set the standard that men adhere to? Women if you start acting like the Queens that you are, and watch you get that King meant for you}. Women stop talking about your baby daddy, because you know when you lay down with dogs you wake up with flees. Women you got to learn to (FLY) F= First, L=Love, and Y= Yourself

Okay, let's get back to respect. Thanks Dad because I learned on my journey to becoming a man, that respect will take you places and open up doors that I would have never imagined. Thanks Dad for planting that seed. Thanks dad for being a man of contents and substances. Thanks for being a man that I and others want to emulate. I got my work cut out for me, but if I could become a portion of the man you are dad. My family, community and the world would be a better place. Thanks dad for never having to go to bed hungry. Thanks dad for keeping clothes on my back, shoes on my feet and a warm place to sleep. Thanks for always being there, and your action showed that you care. I present this day for you to show my appreciation for all you do, so today I would like to create some memories for you to store away. Dad I love you for just being you, and making me a better man, because of your examples I know what it takes to be a man.

Now that I am a parent, I understand the struggles of my parents. I see the struggles of my daughter. One of the qualities that I am working on as a parent is patience and forgiveness. As a parent, I want my children to grasp everything I tell them. I know as a human being and as a parent I cannot control other human beings thoughts and/or their actions. Nevertheless, as a parent I do want to be in control. It is in a man's DNA to want to protect and control the things that he loves. I do not know if the word control is the appropriate term; being that we live in a political correct society. I will exchange the word control to influence or maybe guide them to make positive choices. Yeah, that sounds much better. Raising a child is not an easy task, if I had a choice between being a rocket scientist and a parent; I'll try my hand at being a rocket scientist. No, but on a more serious note. During the Black and I am Proud Power Movement in the sixties and early seventies. My parents would say to me "boy don't let nobody tell you that you ain't nobody, and remember you are a child of God, so that mean you "ain't" below no man." Another thing they would say, "hold your head up, and be proud of who you are, and just because who you are, you have to work five times harder than they do, and sometimes ten times harder than them." They would always encourage us to be better and to do well in school and get an education. Hell, we can't get some of our kids today to read the writings on the side of a cereal box today. They have too many distractions, and parents are not encouraging them to be their best. They are more concern with dressing to impress, rather than learning to be your best and using money to invest.

Suggestion Moment: Parents let's not allow our children to think that being mediocre or just being average is okay. Let's push them to excel in all their endeavors. One way to do this is to remind our children that all things are possible and the only person can make it impossible is their selves. Affirm to them that the only limitations that they have are the ones that they place on their selves. Parents we have to continue to grow spiritual, physical, and mentally; again we can't just talk the talk and not walk the walk. Our children watch our feet, and not our mouths, in other words they watch what we do and not what we say. Parents we must continue to rebuild what has been torn down, we must continue to reshape, refurbish, and renew ourselves. Parents I ask, how can we show our children strength, hope, and perseverance when we are so easily ready to give up and accept mediocrity ourselves?

My black beautiful people have we gotten so comfortable in our condition of this delusional success, that some parents ignore to pour into their children the ingredients necessary to empower them to dig back into their rich history of their ancestral greatness. They must align themselves with the knowledge of their history, so they can borrow some of the courage and strength to build upon the struggles that our great warriors fought for. This will allow them to carve out their own place in history, and fight the battles that they too will encounter on their journey in life. Parents we have to be diligent in our efforts to do positive things in the presence of our children. We have to be careful what we do in front of them, and how we resolve our disagreements. I say this because I watch my grandson who is three, and he tries to mimic everything he sees his older cousins and other people do. Our children mimic what we do and say, so be conscious of this parents. For the life of our children we have to replace those (tell- a- lie- vision) heroes, and parents we must step up to the responsibilty and be their real life heroes. This is going to take some discipline and dedication to champion the cause of good parenting.

As I began to reflect and appreciate my life, I was thinking about the conversations my wife and daughters were having after church. I was at my daughter Betty's house, and after dinner we all sat around the dinner table having a conversation with Betty's new guy that she was dating. The guy probably though he was in an interrogation room or under FBI investigation. No, really it was not that bad. It made me realize that with all my mistakes. The most important thing was that we talk to each other and continue to be there for each other. They talked about back in the day and how wild I was, and some of the really stupid stuff I did. Despite all those things I did, they still allowed love to prevail and love me despite of me. Now that is a blessing. What I am saying here is that life or parenting does not come with a how to fix it manual. Parents do your very best, and when your children grow up, and you're sitting around the table someday talking about the good old times. Remember parents just do the best parenting you know how, and if it done out of love the miscues of parenting will not look that terrible later down the road. Before I left my daughters house I fix me some of ribs, chicken, string beans and macaroni and cheese to take to work. After I put my food in the car, I went back into the house and hug all my daughters and told them I loved them. That moment and what I was feeling at the time is priceless. Nope, you can't put a dollar price on this moment, and these were my moment to have and to cherish. You can't rob me of this moment X factors.

You may have succeeded with my son but I still got joy. Glory! In that moment, I began to ponder on the thoughts that my son and I were robbed of so many memories. Those manufactured X factors took our priceless moments. Where are you son? Daddy heart cries out to you. I love you son, and I am still out here fighting to get my chance to tell you man to man of those silent tears I cry. Sorry son you deserved so much more than what was given to you. Your parents' never gave you a chance to flourish and to be all that you could be. We clipped your wings, and you never learned how to fly.

Chapter 6

Frustration!

Frustration comes when I am hopeless, because of my constant oppression. Hope is what keeps me motivated to wake up the next day. That is the motivational factor that sustains the human being inside of me. I'm hoping that there is a brighter tomorrow, and that a breakthrough is on the way. Frustration comes when I witnessed a young single mother struggling to get her baby off to daycare on the public transit system, and the young man that's getting on the bus beside her does not have enough love and respect to assist her with lifting the baby's stroller onto the bus.

What frustrates me is my people have accepted it as normal to have fatherless homes, which is as unnatural as shooting hormones into little chicks, and making them full grown chickens in three days. What frustrates me is my people have accepted black men killing black men as the norm. This is as unnatural as lynching was to black people. What frustrates me is that this justice system we are subjected to has made it acceptable for white police officer (new KKK) to vent their frustration by killing black boys, black men, and black women whenever they feel the urge to vent. Then they have the nerves to tell us we will see that justice is done, but they are the ones who investigate themselves, and when they do administer their version of justices it is done in such a clandestine matter. We march and we shout, but nothing changes because they got the law and the guns in their possession. All we got is division, churches and wine stores, and barbershops, and killings and more killings. This is frustration every day the same shit. If this shit doesn't unite us nothing will. United we fall and divided we stand; this real talk!

I'm terrified and frustrated as a father, as grandfather, and as a man that I have absolutely no power to protect my young grandbabies from the laws and the injustice that awaits them. I know from my own personal experiences that because of the melanin in their skin they will be harassed because of a belief system that feeds off of treating and viewing those of a darker hue with a different set of lenses. Am I so afraid of the white man laws that I have turned both cheeks? I won't even fight for my babies lives, so that they can have rights and dignity as human beings. God said or his prophets, scribes or somebody said during the biblical era something like" turn the other cheek, but after I turn the other cheek what do I turn? Man I tired of all this bullshit, the police killing us; the court system killing us; poverty killing us, and us killing us. And on Sunday all I get is the struggle won't last always, your break through is coming. Sew a seed of just one hundred dollars and watch what God going to do for you. Man/ Women/ Black/ White/ Jew/ Gentile whoever; God it's been over 500 something years, and my peoples are still waiting. Where you at man! Come holler at brother when you can?

Wake up! Wake up! Wake Up! My people will perish for their lack of knowledge. What frustrates me is when I speak of my history my own people are shunning it, and telling me I am a radical. All I want to do is restore us back to productive, prideful, honorable, loving, and respectful people, because that is who we are. The truth is the light and the way. Here's where the mental illness comes into play. We will love and accept everyone's culture, but look down upon our own as if it is something vile. We need help as a people; before are complete extinction occurs. Take a look at all the black nations around the world and the horrific conditions they are forced to live under. If you care to, look at the health disparities, wealth disparities, criminal justices disparities, and education disparities. We "ain't" got time for foolishness. Wake Up! Wake up! Wake Up! Those who believe we have advanced and got something in this land; tell me what we got that is sustainable to pass down to our children? Tell me? What have we produce that's going make the world a better place for our children? Please don't say we got famous entertainers, basketball stars, and rappers/ singers. Most of them are caught up in a system too, and are just as fucked up as the rest of us. Ignorant is ignorant no matter what address you live at Beverly Hills or the inner city on 117th St. Clair Street.

Being the dad to four precious daughters, my frustration is real, and as their dad I cannot protect these natural nurturing emotional loving young women from the wolves (men). I question my parenting skills. Have I provided them with the survival tools to fend off the emotional turmoil from the attacks of the wolves (men)? I get frustrated because I know that relationship are difficult, and that their chances of finding that special man that understands his role as a man is to love her and protect her will be a challenge. Not to disrespect and neglect her. The other day one of my daughters invited me over to dinner, and she began tell me about the relationship of a male friend of hers. She showed me a posting on Facebook of him giving other female flowers, and another girl warning my daughter of the dangers that awaits her with this man. She also presented to me a statement that he made to another female that was incriminating. This statement alone was evidence that he was trying to get those panties or already got those panties. Finally, she would pose this question to me, "daddy why men have to be so dishonest?" In the back of my mind I'm thinking who the fuck am I to answer that question? I don't know shit about honesty. Here's the heart crusher for me. She said, "Daddy I go into relationships expecting to get hurt." My heart cried out, and I realized at that moment the damage men inflict upon the spirit of a woman. My God! My God! My God! Help us disobedient, lying, cheating bastard get well.

I am so frustrated right now when I see so many of my beautiful black women who are loved deprived, and are too eager to be loved. They are so loved starved that they are willing to accept any man as long as he stands upright on two legs. The pool of eligible men is decreasing, and the ones who are available have choices like apples in a barrel. He can leave one and go to another and another. Men and women we are social and sexual beings, and sex once you have engaged in it; like a drug addiction the person will do anything to obtain it. It creates irrational thinking and it is like the heart muscle, it is an involuntary muscle that the human body has no control over. That is why it hard to tell teenager, young adults, and middle age people not to engage in sex, because as humans we have an innate drive to engage in this euphoric activity. Especially, in today's time where it seems like everything revolves around three things sex, money, and violence. Here we have a culture that says to our children don't have sex and if you do be responsible, but our children have not seen examples of healthy sexual relationships. The divorce rate are increasing because children can view famous celebrities' divorces twenty to thirty times in a twenty-four hours news cycle; therefore, reinforcing to our babies that it is fashionable and accepted to be divorced. The same goes for children having babies and not having a father to raise them. I do not believe that having morals, respect, and values for life; should ever be put on the back burner of society' mind. Too many things are out of order and too many people are turning a blind eye to these problems. The blame game is taking place; it's the churches fault; it's the community fault; it's the parents fault, but in reality and the truth be told it's everyone's dam fault that do not lift a finger to try to make changes. People it is time to stop the blame game, and get off the sidelines and get into the game to make a change, because it is our precious children dying and are babies being cattle off into the Prison Industry Complex.

Solution Moment: American Society as a whole has become a place where T.V and gadgets, and other people sound bites on the radio and other media outlets have literally taken over their ability to think. This New America has become a bunch of individualized walking Attention Deficit Disorder (ADD), and Attention Deficit/Hyperactivity Disorder (ADHD) robots. Furthermore, they have become morally bankrupt, and influence by Hollywood and lack the ability to discern what is morally human for the good of all mankind. Here is my idea of how to use the manufactured X factors for the good of mankind. This highly commercialized society whose ideas are transmitted into their brains by these powerful dispensers of information. By the way most Americans are limited to only 10% of brain capacity.

Americans have their holidays that they celebrate, but some of them have no significant purpose, and most of them have lost their relevancy. I believe if the American people can unplug from their gadgets there may be a slight chance of restoring our ability to feel and think again. With this miraculous ability to think again, they could advocate for a holiday that can and will have a positive impact in their lives. Now attempt to expand the 10% brain capacity, and grasp this idea that

would improve the family structure. There may be those in certain industries that would certainly lobby against this idea, and this is where the ability to think will have to be engaged.

I propose that citizens of the United States unite to have a day to recognize and celebrate marriage. What will this do to change the image of marriage? This will shift the negative connotation of marriage, and create a new narrative for marriage. This will attract people to have the desire to get married. The powers to be of course will have to promote and commercialize it, so that they can prosper off of it too. Hell, we can make as big as Christmas or the Mardi Gras in New Orleans. This new found holiday would have an immediate impact in the communities around the United States and its families. They could even provide tax incentives for ever year after five years of marriage. Marriage would become an attraction rather than a death sentence. Call your senators now. (Laughing, it would never fly because that would mean Congress would have to work with each other, and as long as there is a President in the <u>White House</u> with melanin in office you can forget about anything good happening for the working citizens of the United States. Okay, it was just wishful thinking people. Don't shoot the messenger.

Let me open your third eye on some real shit. The black man was emancipated supposedly when Lincoln freed the slaves on January 1, 1863 or on when Congress passed and ratified the Thirteenth Amendment December 6, 1865. This is where that beat us at with that slick ass pen, and create their wealth under the disguise of their laws; again in which they created. The Thirteenth Amendment reads like this: Section 1. Neither slavery nor involuntary servitude, **except as a punishment for a crime wherefore the party shall have been duly convicted**, shall exist within the United States, or any place subject to their jurisdiction

Section 2: Congress shall have power to enforce this article by appropriate Legislator

Readers research and find out what happen after "we'gat fre". I want the reader to do some work, and learn to seek truth, and not just accept my word or those thirty second sound bites and those talking heads on the(tell -a -lie- vision). Black folks we can become what we once were, and that was people of courage and critical thinkers.

January 9, 2015, while working on my book I took my grandbabies to the world premiere to see the movie Selma:

I am frustrated that the movie theater did not have a line of people waiting to get in; like the lines they have when Michael Jordan comes out with a new tennis shoe. It is not often that a movie of this magnitude is allowed to be made here in America. It reaffirmed the disconnection between the powerless and the elite in America and around the world. This is not a movie about black and white it is a movie about injustice and terrorism in America against its American citizens. My frustration was enhanced while viewing the movie, because the monstrous battle that they were fighting in the sixties could very well parallel to today. Many of the exact struggles black's are facing today with police brutality and economic disparities. This movie is about courageous people who decided that they whether die with dignity than live like animals. People this is a ploy that they are still using to keep the poor fighting amongst themselves. All while the gap continues to expand among the haves and the haves not, and the citizens are connived into voting for sound bites. Police are killing the poor, and people of color under the protection of laws. I was inspired by this movie to do more for myself, family, and my community. The underlining issues during that time was the disadvantage in America were being denied their God given rights, and they were willing to sacrifice their lives for the freedom and liberty that America promised them, so that all Americans could enjoy the spoils of freedom.

Civil Right Movement was more than wanting to sit next to a white person on a bus or drink out of the same drinking fountain. No, these disenfranchised people wanted a share of the resources, power, and the responsibility that came along with real freedom. The Civil Rights movement was one of the many expression and desires for real freedom. The question for the reader has black folks gain power? Have the working class gained economic freedom? Are the resources readily available for all Americans to share or do a select few control the resources? I just want my readers to do a little thinking, because with the modern gadgets the ability to think is becoming extinct for the fast moving instance microwave society. The Americans are allowing those manufactured X factors to make us a bunch dummies; where we can't think beyond the narrative that is provided. Fred Foxx from Stanford & Son said it best, "you dummy."

Here is a prime example of the foolish stuff that the manufactured X factor wants us to believe. The manufactured X factors want to place a bull's-eye on the rap industry, and target that genre of music specifically as the sole entity to all the causes of our children negative behaviors. Nevertheless, they negate to widen the scope to include that they are closing more schools in the inner cities and building prisons. However, they can find it in their budget to spend billions of dollars to invest in more prisons. Do you think this is happening by coincidence? They need to widen their lenses to include: violent movies, violent video games, poverty, working poor, unequal distribution of resources, oppression, suppression, depression, cultural conditioning, social inequalities, food inequalities, health inequalities, military policing, regression of the voting rights act, environmental issues, and a plethora of other issues seen and unseen. They want to blame and put a microscope solely on rap music; oh and by the way they control that too. Hell, can they control my pay check, and start by paying me a livable wage. I have worked so hard to change my life and become a better person. No, let me rephrase that; God changed my life. Nevertheless, with that being said, I get depressed and frustrated over my financial status. Man, this poverty plays on my psychic, because I'm working but on pay day all my money goes towards bills, and I can't get ahead. I am working pay check to pay check. **Well, I wrote a poem about what here?**

Poem: Can I get paid?

I don't mean to make no fuss, but this job thing got my life all messed up it's like I am still riding on the back of the bus. This job got my life in an uproar, because I'm tired of being classified as the working poor. If I'm going to go to work and still be poor; then what the heck am I working for?

It seems the more hours I work, the less I make. And the more they decide to take.

People when are we going to get our tax break?

I go to work every day and I still can't gain any wealth, And beside they don't even want to pay for my health. Brothers this job got my life in a wreck, because I'm just like all the rest of the 46 million Uninsured I'm living pay check to pay check.

I've been in the cheese lines, welfare lines, unemployment line, and now they got me standing in the check cashing advance line. Gas prices are sky high and I can barely getting by.

Maybe this is why my brothers and sisters turn to dope, because they just don't see any hope. People it's time for us to come to the realization that were all in the same boat, and we're hanging on by a very very thin rope. We're all trying to live that American dream by working that 9 to 5, but we're barely staying alive and are j.o.b. keeps us <u>just over broke</u>.

I got a job, but I swear to you on pay day, it seems like I'm being strong armed robbed. Brothers and sisters this job got my life in a wreck; I'm tired of living pay check to pay check. And in the words of Fanny Lou Hammer I'm sick of tired of being sick and tired…. of being sick and tired of being sick and tired of working pay check to pay check.

Oh well, let me go to work so I can get a pay check.

The frustration comes when the wicked oppressor controls the narrative that poor people do not want to improve upon their dire economic conditions. I beg to differ, because I have seen strong black single mothers work two jobs while attending college at night. Only to be burden with an enormous financial debt, and the only relief she receives is on Sunday morning in church where that elusive hope is offered for few hours to give her the strength to carry on. The Lord knows she needs all the strength she can get to deal with the enemy(X factors).

I'm frustrated to learn that the manufactured X factors have disenfranchised more than 400,000 non-violent black men who have been imprisoned for over indicted charges, and now that they have serve the (PIC) time they should have the rights to exercise their rights as a free men to vote. Yet, they are denied their God give right to be a man and cast a vote in the land of the free. Once they are freed from the criminal justice system, they should have the same rights as any other citizen; therefore, their rights should be reenacted. Their rights should be restored to elect an official who will address their concerns. Why would they not want them to vote? In the movie Selma it enlightened the importances of voting. When they did gain their right to vote, and they exercised their votes they were able vote a racist Klu Klux Clansmen Bull O' Conner out of office. Maybe that is why states are suppressing and amending new laws to hinder black people from voting in elections. They are turning the hands of time, and erasing the efforts that millions of blacks and whites died for to see that all Americans have a chance to participant in a Democratic voting process. Here's a reality check: Do you know that it has only been fifty years since we were allowed to cast a ballot at the voting booth in America? Now they are trying to turn back the progress that has been made with these new voting restriction and requirements. There has never been anything wrong with the voting process before; now all sudden there is a dire need for voting reform.

My frustration comes when I see my people drawing the correlation to being poor to acting poor; meaning to act poor is to have no self worth and so you do self destructive things to yourself and to their communities and families. Sad to say, but that is a mental illness.

I get frustrated because all the pieces of the puzzle were there for my son to have a fighting chance. He had the foundation, because he had grandparents who came from that old style of parenting. Being in the presence of my mother, you could feel the love that radiated from her, and she had a way of drawing you into that place of love. My son never got to experience her love, so sad for him.

The people spoke highly of my mom at her funeral, "said that they felt her loving presence, and that she had such a comforting spirit." My dad is a disciplinary figure of a man who instilled in me work ethics. He would often say these adages: "If a man doesn't work he doesn't eat." It' takes more than one way to skin a cat," If you make your bed hard you got to lay in it." "Keep your nose clean, so that way you won't have to be looking over your back," My dad did not drink, gamble, and did not do things that would be detrimental to him. My dad opened up the world to me. Our family would travels to various states to our family reunions, and we would go every year when were children. My dad exposed me to a world that expanding beyond the neighborhood street corners. Had I not gotten that foundation, maybe I would have allowed the streets to totally consume me, but because I had something to compare the streets to, which I knew was wrong. I had the morals and the memory of what was right, which my dad imbued in me at an early age.

In the realm of things, as a parent I often felt powerless knowing that no matter what method I attempted to convince my daughters that my way is the way to promise land. My frustration comes to reality when I cannot protect my very own children from the very evils that enthralled them. I want my children to be exempted from having to experiences the realities of life. I want them to skip the bad stuff the heart aches, the financial pit falls, and failures. Unfortunately, that would not be the case for my precious baby girls.

I want to build a fence around them, and only allow what is good for them to enter. I get frustrated when my words of wisdom fall on death ears. That is when I have to reflect to my own youthful days, and realize that I did the very same thing and worse. I absolutely did not adhere to the words of my parents. I often wish I had, maybe I would have avoided some of the lumps and bruises along the way to maturity.

Note to myself- 10/25/14 Talk about the struggles and frustration that led me to be the parent I am today and intertwine those ideas, knowing that I was unable to have an influence in my son's life. Tell of my experience of being told by the magistrate that I could not have visitation rights to see my son; even though I was in compliance with the laws of the land, and with CSEA. Share your silent tears with the world. Explain to the world the term "Fatherless Father". A fatherless father is me, which is a father who is a father but was not allowed to be a father. I wanted to coin a phrase that would

identify us fatherless fathers. I wanted a term that would contrast this popularized "deadbeat dead" term that has become associated with fathers; that label is not befitting to all fathers. It does the fatherless father a great injustice, as many of the descriptions of black males often does. It is a play on words, which is something those in the media and politics are familiar with those clever tactics to present something a certain way, so that it has a desired effect. I wanted something that would separate us from that negative connotation, and display a more compassionate term. The "dead beat dad" term just make dad's sound hostile and not worthy of being a father.

I would fall victim to others opinions about being a "dead beat dead", I bought into the public perceptions' about being worthless. It was not until I came to the realization about other people's opinions. That everyone has an opinion and everyone has a butt hole, and just like a butt hole don't nothing but shit comes out of it. I learned that the only opinion that counts is the opinion that I have of myself. When I changed the perception of how I felt about me; things start turning around for me. This hope thing I speak about is a dangerous thing in a good way. I starting having hope, I began to believe that I could accomplish stuff, and I start setting goals. I stop fearing, and start doing. Those things in which I feared I began to cast aside. I began to put my positive thought into perpetual motion, which went out into the universe. I learned that my real wealth was learning to love myself.

God decided to use me, so I was able to stop allowing Danita and her mom and those X factors to rent space in my head for free. That anger and self-destructive behavior would cease to exist. In June of 1998, I would become free from the bondage of myself, drugs and other mind altering substances. I would discover a new way to live.

One day, on my lunch break at the Plating Company, I starting thinking about all the stuff I've been through.(What was the stuff you been through)? Did God give me another chance to get things right just to work in a factory the rest of my life? What did God what me to do? I have always enjoyed school. As a matter of fact, I've been to almost every kind of school; from cooking school to nursing and everything in between, but was not able to complete any of them because of my stinking thinking, and that monkey I carried on my back.

More importantly, I promised my mom on her dying bed, as she took her last breath that I would complete my journey. You see she had seen my many failed attempts to do better, but I never could complete any of my goals. The disease of alcoholisms would not allow me to succeed that sucker is powerful, cunning, and baffling. I could not let her down again. I remember that day; I was sitting beside her in the living room and in that sweet low angelic voice, "Son promise me one thing that you finish school." "I replied in the emotions of that moment with tears flowing from my eyes. Yes mom you bet I will." I really did not know if I would or not, but just to appease her on her dying bed I would say anything. It wasn't until the funeral, while I was listening to the preacher, "if you love your mother then take that love in which she had, and let her love shine in you and let it be a light until the world." Those words went down into the core of my spirit and I took those inspiring words from the preacher, and I "ain't" let my light dim yet; it's still shining. I hope and pray that these words I write in this book reach and inspire my son, who I have never had an opportunity to shine my light on.

Even though things were starting to turn around for me, and I was reaping some of the fruits of my labor. There was still this one area in my life that seems to be cursed, and it was very frustrating. I find it frustrating when the man has the qualities that a woman says she wants, and the man finds a woman that exemplifies all his desires. The relationship in the beginning had all the tools and the making of a fairytale ending. I met this fine ass woman and she had all the attributes a brother was seeking. She was intelligent, beautiful, humorous, caring, and a long list of other great qualities. The problem I encountered was those grown ass disrespectful bebe bebe kids. How can you be with a woman when her kids totally disrespect her? What you think they will do to me? They would dump the grandkids off without notification; no concerns at all with what moms got planned. They would leave the babies and go in the streets probably going to make more babies, so mom can take care of them too. My girl would come home from working two jobs, and I would go by to see her only to find her cleaning and scrubbing the housing. She would clean up behind grown ass want to be adults. She would cook for them; clean for them; and raise her bebe grand babies too. Here is the topping on the cake, and this made me take off like the Jamaican track star Usain Bolt. They would use those four letter words when they spoke to the women I cared for, and I was not cut from that clothe. I knew I could not stand by and let those grown ass bebe kids disrespect her. Men if you are every in that situation get the fuck out, because I ain't about let no funking loud mouth child disrespect me. Women sometimes will get a good man, but cannot keep him because of the children interference. Man that relationship was crazy, I don't know, I guess I did some stupid stuff for the sake of lust and some good pussy.

You know what I learned that some situation you ain't going to change and you can't change, so keep it moving. Sometime even when those heartstrings keep pulling you in; you got cut those heartstrings and use your brain. Now I know it ain't easy, but at some point you got to cut the heartstrings and move on. We are all going to endure some pain, because that is part of the territory of life. Now misery is not part of life that is a choice we make as humans. See misery is staying in something you know ain't right, but you stay in it for the sake of hoping the pain will ease. What happens is you become addicted to drama, and that crazy ass mind of mine will start to believe that drama is a necessity for life. I was literally emotional and spiritually bankrupt from continuously damaging and emotionally scarring God's gift to world (The Black Queen of all life's existences on earth). They should be revered by all; not just black men.

I had to relieve myself from all that craziness that I had created. God was not going to continue to stand by and allow me to harm his beautiful creations. God spoke to my soul and I decline to sign a new contract for my teacher assistance position. I moved out of my apartment, and moved to North Carolina. Where I had no job, and no inclination as to where I would live. The only thing I knew was what God had told me. God told me to free myself of the infliction of my own desires, and strip yourself of your selfish heartless ways by giving up all your worldly possession. I had become emotional distraught, and my conscious had been weighing me down. God knew that he would take something drastic to capture my attention, and to transform a selfish boy into a man of God and character. This leap of faith would lead me on a journey that would change my life and my perspective on life, and would teach me to value my life. By valuing my life, I can value others lives and help them appreciate this gift of life that I took for granted. I would learn on this self discovery journey the understanding of being: Homeless, Joblessness, and Indigent, and as a result of this I learned to be humble. This was a word and something I knew nothing of, which stripped me of this false pride and selfish ways. It change my ways of apathy, to having empathy for my fellow man. I became not only a better man through my six years of spiritual renewal, but a better human and was now able to contribute to the world from the lenses of God's eyes that he allowed me to borrow to see the needs of others.

I no longer blame the women for caring and wanting to share their love with me. I stop looking at myself as the innocent victim. I stop making excuses that only women should have standards, so that men could be more responsible. I now realized that it was a two way street, and that men had the same and maybe even more responsibility to set and have standards when establishing a relationship with women; it not solely her responsibility. I became a man of character and morals, because that what God transformed me into, it would no longer be about pleasing the Mr. Dick anymore. It was about cultivating, building up and making my woman feel loved, respected, and protected by her man. No more silly Coco pops games, because Tricks are made for kids. My God turned a mess into a messenger.

CHAPTER 7

Mental State

Mental Illness: According to Dr. George N. McNeil and Dr. Stephen M. Soreff they describe Psychosis as this: A major disturbance in perceiving and dealing with reality characterized by disordered thinking, bizarre behavior, and extremes of affect, delusions, and hallucinations

The most common diagnosis I am seeing today is anxiety that leads to depression. It leads to depression because most often it is not dealt with at the anxiety level. It can become mind boggling and difficult when a person is constantly in a situation of: oppression, suppressions, poverty, violence, drugs, lack of fundamental education, health care, and living under an unequal justice system, and being attack by police officer. The laws of the land itself are enough for a person to have a mental lapse. Imagine living in a violent, hostile, and angry environment all the time, and the people are always in a survival mode. Having that feeling like it's me against the world (TUPAC), "I got nothing to lose, because it's me against the world,"

The media talks about children in the Middle East and the Gaza Strip, and devastation that they endure on a daily. Which is awful, and no child should have to live under those circumstances. However, I do not believe in all fairness that the Inner cities children should be excluded from that narrative. They too are living in Urban War Zones, where violence plagues their world. However, when it comes to our children they are viewed as evil monster, and deserve to be hunted and shot down by the new KKK, because of an environment over thrown by violence, drugs, crime, and injustices. I would ask the media to venture into these urban war zones, and take a subjective view of these victims. Where violence has become the norm; they have become desensitized to the gun shots and the dead bodies. This type of daily and negative environment would cause a psychosis to most human minds. **Here is a poem to take a glimpse into the world of our children:**

Lost Innocence

Life in the box called the hood where little children have become hard, cold, and insensitive towards death. They play in crack infested streets where dead bodies replace the chalk lines that were once used to play games like hopscotch.

They play in playgrounds plagued with HIV and needles, and bullets shot that rains out like rain falling from the sky. I witness these atrocities and I ask God why?

They have learned to weather the storm and bullets shots in the hood have become the norm. They don't even flitch when the bullets ring out throughout the hood.

Their young conversations are not of the lessons of school, but of the harden lives that they have lived in such a brief time on this earth known as the hood. Where everything in their existences is of no good, and that just the way it is in the hood. Little Tommy tell his dreams of reaching the age of 25. These are the dreams they dream in the hood; instead of these precious gifts from god dreaming of becoming doctors, lawyers, scientist; their dreams are of growing old at the ripe age of 25.

These innocent souls have witness more deaths than a soldier at war; because where they live they are casualties of war in a war zone commonly known as the hood. Their misconception of life is standing in front of abandon buildings claiming their hoods. Killing each other over land which they have no deeds to, because they got nothing better to do.

Their forced to live with this exterior toughness from what they've witness in movies and videos. Now their disrespecting women and calling them hoes. Because TV has taken the place of parenting because mommy is working two jobs and daddy is in jail for selling dope. And because of him the entire family is in disarray, hanging on by a thin rope.

The world has passed them by, because every time you turn on the TV what do you see? Well, you see them talking about wars and hunger or how they've spent millions of dollars towards humanity for the sake of good, but those same innocent children are still dying in the hood.

What happen to the days when kids were able to play in the hood, because it was all good in the hood as we over stood? Back then you could look out from your windows and see the future of hope.

Kids would be outside riding their bikes; girls playing hopscotch; boys running to see who could run like Jessie Owens or Carl Lewis.

Who would have imagined today our kids on every street corner selling dope?

Back then we played hard and had lots of fun, because we knew when the streets lights came on we were done.

The street lights today represent dead bodies and chalk lines of lives that once lived in the hood. God I ask just one thing, can you make the hood all good so that these innocent souls can have the life they deserve and should?

--"Peace" Just a little bit of love is all we need. 2007 the Messenger

-Oh, and by the way, I failed to clarify earlier who the new KKK is. They are just as effective as when they were first established. The only differences are today there more subtle, and have changed their attire from the white hoodies to: Black robes, pin stripe suits on the senate and house of representative, and congress floors of the Whitehouse. They wear blue uniforms, and they put their hands on bibles and swear to serve and protect all. These are some of the manufactured X factors our people are challenged with. The one thing for sure is our children are dying from the hands of the law and from other children who look just like them. Here in the twenty first century the media outlets around the world continue to portray black men in a negative criminal way. Displaying them to be more violent minded to criminal activities. This creates a world that is able to desensitize the murdering of people of the darker hue, because they view them as less than human. They can now rationalize the vicious treatment of black people as normal. This negative stereotypes' of Black people reminds me of the movie produced by D.W. Griffin in the 1915, "Birth of a Nation," where he depicted black men with tails running around rapping white women. This sparked an outrage in society, and increased the violence by the KKK, causing people to riot throughout the United States of America. Now fast-forward to 2014, with the increase of violent acts upon African American from the new KKK, the men in blue. Doing this demonic era blacks were deemed as rapist and animalistic creature that were not human like white folks. Fast-forward to today blacks are still marching and beating to the same drum. Now they are polarized as thugs, lazy, and a danger to their society. Black's are still trying be validated by what white men consider the norm. {These children witness some horrifying things, and their environment, social, and biological influences affects the way they perceive the world, and their state of mind.}This is the results of the sociopolitical implications of oppression where you have the ethnocentric monoculture group that their beliefs are: superiority, others are inferior, can impose standards that others must live by and can create institutions. These individual wears an invisible veil, and this dominant culture is allowed easier access to privileges ("White privilege"). They may view minority groups as pathological. There is another dilemma here in America and abroad, and that is the clash of racial realities. Whose reality is the true reality? Oftentimes, the perceptions held by the dominant group differ significantly from those of the marginalized groups. While the disempowered group is more likely to be accurate, it is the group in power that has the ability to define reality. The perception of how one feels about themselves and those images that are displayed, that are supported by numerous outlets around the world confirming what you have learned to believe; that you have no self-worth. This opens up the door for self-hate and self destruction. Yes, we have made progress in the United States of America, but have we accepted the individualism of the Europeans', and deserted the collectiveness of our talents to achieve more. I guess my question is can Black men and women do more or have they reached the zenith of their progress? **Here's my solution moment:** Yes, of course there are still many institutional challenges black people face. My suggestions are let's change the immediate things that we can change, and then we can conquer the external factors. Black people can start by no longer accepting the victim role, and stop being an easy target for the world to prey on us. Stop allowing the world to dictate how you feel about yourselves, and restore that black dignity. Black people must start the rigorous cycle of learning to love their selves. Once that process has begun, then they can take their talents and resources and use them for the empowerment of creating for self. Again don't feel guilty, for trying to enhance your people and lift your brother up along with you. Black people can make it a **we** thing, and not an individual thing we can get this thing called love and unity. The result will be a real voice in the political system: legal system, health system, and quality schools. This will open opportunity for the other entities necessary to be a free people who can cast their will upon their people.

Here are some suggestions to improve our economical dependency. This is not an original ideal this plan has been expressed by: Marcus Garvey, Dr. King, Dr. Farrah Gray, Malcolm X, Minister Louis Farrakhan, Professor Griff, and countless others. We cannot start off with an enormous ideal like Bill Cosby and try to buy NBC, so that we can have our views expressed. No because of our mental psychosis as a nation of people we have to take tiny baby steps to secure our economic future to create generational wealth. Hell might have to crawl, but al lease we are making an effort. Black folks let us begin with organizing our celebrities and those of us who have achieved wealth can buy into investing into the black community one block at a time. How can they do that? By purchasing grocery stores, gas stations, abandon houses in their own neighborhoods. This will have a far greater impact than a recreation center or a toy give away around Christmas. This will create jobs for us by us. We can call it **Building**

a Nation One Block at a Time. Then we can begin to expand into banking, schools, hospitals, cultural centers, libraries, beauty products, and manufacturing. Don't say we cannot do it, because it has been done with the Black Wall Street. Black folks we have a blue print, but because of the disconnection with our history, as to who we are, and where we want to go, we don't know how to get there. Black folks are like a ship at sea without a compass to guide their moral consciousness. They're out there going where every the wind blows with no directions and no destination. How long will the lost be able to stay out there at sea without direction to shore? Black folks have been depleted of self, so they find themselves in no better position than they were doing slavery, because black folks continue to allow their children to be unplugged from their history. Their history is the fuel that will provide them with the knowledge that will enrich and empower them. Therefore, they must immediately stop allowing the manufactured X factors to validate their existence. They must negate those negative images that the world sees, and exploit their positive attributes and make that the news of the day. Don't believe the hype we have more positive contributions, and are doing positive thing in our families and communities, but the interpretation gets buried on the back pages with the obituary section in small print, where one needs a magnifying glass to read it. For those of us that do know, we got to share that information by any means necessary. We got to take the mental chains off, because our history shouldn't be a mystery.

Black folks maybe we need to act like it's a funeral every day, because it appears that this is the only time I am witnessing unity. That is the unfortunate truth that we only coalesce when tragedy is at our doorsteps. Sorry, I have to apologize because that is not the only time black folks come together. We will unite at the nightclubs, sporting events and at our churches. If we could only reverse this mind set, and replace it with a dose of love and care for one another like the true people of God that we are? Our purpose and accomplishments would be unlimited.

CHAPTER 8

Robbed of Fatherhood

The Justice Hall in Detroit, the day was October 10, 2014, on a Friday at 1:30 pm. I was dealt another devastating blow to the heart and mind again with the expectation of fulfilling my dream of seeing my son; even if was through the iron prison gates of hell. The tears would flow like rivers right there in front of the sheriffs, and whoever else was there at the prison intake desk. This was the same cry I had when I was told in 2000, that I could not obtain visitation rights by some magistrate who never even allowed me to express myself in the matter. He knew nothing about me nor did he care to know anything about me. He perceived me as just another lazy black man although at the time I was in compliant with their laws, and was gainfully employed at the time of my request for visitation to see my son Arnell. I knew that I had to have all my business in order when I stepped to those folks in black robes.

I finally gather all the information necessary with help of my friend who works in the Sheriff Department. I had made the plans to visit my son in jail, and the waiting was killing me because I had about two weeks before I could take off of work and drive to Cleveland, Ohio. Those were the longest two weeks ever; I don't think I got a good night sleep during those two weeks. My dream of seeing my boy was finally going materialize after all my failed attempts. Nothing could go wrong, because I crossed all my T's and dotted all I's.

This time Danita, her mom, the child support system, no one could prevent this meeting from happening. I was going tell my son I love him, and when he gets out we can talk and build a friendship if he wanted. God finally got around to hearing my prayer, so nothing could go wrong. I was going to get the closure that I needed to mend this void in my heart. I entered the Jail Center earlier because I wanted no slip ups. My scheduled time of 1:00 pm had arrived to see my son. I was going to get some closure on this living hell that I have been living for so long. I walked to the police officer intake booth to sign in for my visitation. "Hi, how are you doing officer?" "Fine, what is your name and who are you here to see?" "My name is Bob, and I am here to see my son Arnell."

"Well, sir I am sorry his mom came and got him yesterday." You mean to tell me he not here anymore? "No, he was released yesterday." I was in a state of damn, this shit can't be happening. What kind of trick was God playing on me? I began looking around for the cameras; because maybe I was on one of those television shows that play tricks on you. This just couldn't be real. After a few minutes, I saw no one appear to tell me that I just got punked. The reality of the moment and what had actually taken place had set in. I had put so much mental effort into this trip to see my son only to be disappointed time after time again.

I just could not control my emotions. I cried me a river. Where do I go from here? I don't have any more answers. I could not call the grandma, because that's who I would have to address my concerns to. I though what the hell; it's worth a try. "Hi, my I speak with Danita." "Who is this? Bob. "What do you want?" "I would like to speak with Danita Please." Angrily as usually, she replied, don't call here Danita move out of town. "Okay, thank you. Before I could tell her to have a blessed day, I heard a loud click and then silence. She hung the phone up; I was not alarmed at that behavior, because I have grown all too familiar with her disposition over the years. But for a split second that old bottled up rage wanted to tell her, "That I hated her for what she has done to our lives, and I hated her for not allowing me to be a father to my damn son, and I hated her for taking my right to give my first born my name". I was really hurting because to want to tell another human being that you hate them is very ungodly.

There is always that piece of hope that maybe this time would be different, but no I got what I have been getting for years. There would be absolutely no bending of her rules at all; she was firm as an Oak tree. There was no palm tree in her because that old devil had no flexibility of compassion for me or anyone else; unless there was an interior gain for her. I did not see any in this case at all. Robbery is when something has been taken from you by force without your permission. I did not provide permission to be eliminated from my natural God' inheritance of fatherhood and the thief should be sentenced befitting to the crime. This is a crime of the most malicious attempt, because its devious purpose is to kill and destroy. I truly felt when I was denied my natural inheritance to be a father to my son, which I had a part in creating. I never had the privilege to help cultivate and nurture something so valuable from God. I never wanted to be a sperm donor, but that was one of those X factors showing up again robbing me of my precious gift of fatherhood. I feel like I have been robbed of an extension of me, so I feel that I will never be complete. The sad part about this entire mess is my son is walking around just like me, and probably feeling confused and incomplete too.

When I left the Justice Hall that day, I really felt emotionally deflated, feeling like life was so unfair but most of all I felt sorry for my son. Who did not ask to be born to Danita and Bob, and to a grandmother that did not allow for an innocent child to be loved by his father and by his father's grandparents? They had so much love to give. He was robbed of a sister, cousin's uncles, and aunties. Who can I press charges on for this life time robbery?

CHAPTER 9

Silent Tears

I had the excuse of alcohol to take away the fact that I was not able to be a father, or a loving and caring individual. See the world was telling me that I did not fit into the picture frame that America wanted me to fit in. I felt my efforts as man was not sufficient for society. I kept seeing and hearing through the eyes of others their perception of me; which became me. I begin to internalize and take on those images projected towards me. My thoughts told me that I was lazy even though I work twelve long hours for slave like wages. I know slaves didn't get paid anything, but with those low wages there was not much of a difference. I was always told if a man doesn't work he doesn't eat. I still couldn't escape the reality of my world no matter how hard I tried. The world would deem my efforts less than average, and I would validate the world's opinions. The encouragement that I was starving for never arrived, so I decided that I would make my own mark as man. All those negative stereotypes of a black man, I was going prove them wrong, but at the time I didn't know who they were so them was everyone in my distorted mind.

The black man wasn't smart enough, the black man were dogs, and to have that confirmed by my black woman. They would tell me that I could do better, so I could be just like the white man. Everything I did had to be in comparison to the white man ideology. But see I could get even with them all, because I had alcohol. When I drank I could be and do anything my mind could conceive. The alcohol had me believing I was; successful, loving, a good father even though I was not there. My mind was playing tricks on me. The thirty dollars I had in my pocket I could buy everyone in the club a round. Waking up the next morning broke mentally, and feeling the impact of my disillusioned mind. Where do I get off at in a world that what's to label me a deadbeat dad, and make me feel like I was 3/5 of a man? I was tired of hearing you could be anything you want in this world if you tried, sometimes I couldn't get them words out my fuckin head. This feeling of inadequacy of not measuring up or maybe it was me not believing I could try, and if I did try? I would only fall short just like all the other times. Yes, those half attempts to do something worthwhile in my life, and to prove to the world that I was a whole human being and not just 3/5 of a man. I feared success because self pity and failure was a better option, because that meant that I did not have to put any effort to change. Change meant doing something different and different meant that I would probably have to stop using mind altering drugs to escape reality. That meant I had to put the drugs and alcohol to rest and face life's test. The task of change I did not welcome with open arms.

Every time I would summon that beam of hope, here comes that dam addiction jumping on my back weighing me down again and robbing me of hope. I would return to my sick and twisted delusional world, that I was somebody important, and everyone else needed to get their lives in order. See I worked an entire eight hours, and I got thirty dollars in my pocket after taxes. I had enough for a pack a cigarette, a fifth of some rot gut wine, and a cheap hooker with my twenty dollar crack rock. So don't you point your righteous holier than thy finger at me, because I am a man? I earn my own money to get high, because I don't owe anybody anything. If I want to spend my hard earn money getting high I could. It's your fault and the worlds fault, so don't blame me for my actions. Now back the fuck up, before you get fucked up. Why anybody care about what I do? If I hurting anybody it's me, so won't everybody just get off my back, and quit telling me what I could have been. I could have been a million things, but I am not. I do what I know best so I stagger to Mr. Brown's store and get me a shorty of MD 20/20, to bring me down from tweaking off that crack. Next thing I know, I awaken in the fourth district jail shivering cold and bleeding from the lip. I am shaking like a crap game, because I am coming to my senses, and I don't know where the blood came from or why I was in jail. That is what I later discovered is called a blackout. That is a hell of place to be in; not knowing why you are in jail and you got blood all over you. To God I give the Glory for taking me out of the darkness into marvelous light, and relieving me from this disease of alcoholism!

I owe so many people an apology. I could write a book on my apologies alone. God brought me out of the hell fire of addiction, and restored my appreciation for life and showed me the value of the people I have in my life. I realize that I was not only hurting myself, but this disease affected so many other peoples' lives that I love. I cause an awful lot of pain, and burn down plenty of bridges on my journey to self- destruction.

Here is my heartfelt apology in my poem:

SILENT TEARS

Dad forgive me for all the pain that I have burdened you with, but most of all forgive me for the many nights that you have cried those silent tears. Mom forgive me for not fulfilling your expectations, and hurting you during my dark days of alcohol and drug addiction, but most of all forgive me for the many nights you have cried those silent tears.

Forgive me my precious daughter for not being there. To show you how much I care, but most of all forgive me for the many nights you have cried those silent tears. Forgive me for every woman that I ever hurt because of my womanizing, but most of all forgive me for the many nights you have cried those silent tears.

Silent tears are those tears too heart wrenching to cry out loud. These tears are cried alone. Silent tears are tears cried in the dark of the night, when the heart and mind are one. Please forgive me for those silent tears.

There comes a point and time in everyman's life that he has to make a decision whether that decision is to improve and try to make things better, or remain in the self-destructive poor me why me mentality. That self pity and self doubt had to be lifted. It will take a power greater than my own understanding and limited intelligence, to relieve me of my own insanity and restore me back to sanity. Whatever a man decides to do once he has come to that point in his life where he has to look at his reality, and must decide for himself what path is he is going to take, and in that moment of clarity he chooses which direction he's going to travel. He will choose to travel the road where light and hope can be found, or take the dark road that often leads to complete misery and hopelessness. Every man will come to this point in his life where he will have to choose his own destiny.

It is a terrible road to travel, because I have travelled that dark lonely road searching and seeking, but never finding anything other than more of the same misery and hopelessness. I am seeking, but what is it that I seek? That is a dangerous place to be, when a man begins to entertain the thoughts of being in the pits of hell as more inviting than the joy of life and all that life has to offer. I want to inspire the readers to take the path of hope it will be a struggle indeed, but the journey will eventually lead to that destination of hope, and once a man gains hope he suddenly realizes that the impossible ain't so impossible anymore. Now that his confidence as a man has been restored, he takes the steering wheel and he drives to his own destination. He realizes the only limitations that he has are the ones he places upon himself.

That was exactly what happened to me, I stop looking outside of myself to find myself. I started searching for positive influences, so I reach out to those books and memories I had of positive African American men. I began to equip myself with the tools needed to become a man of character. I read books on my history other than what was provided to me in school. I began to ask questions about who I was as a black boy early on in life, so the foundation was implanted in me. I would read for hours, because I was fascinated with how black folks would not succumb to the horrific conditions that they were subjected to. Because my great ancestors overcame, I too believe I could overcome. Their impossible made it possible today for me to triumph in the face of adversity. My knowledge of my history provided me with the courage to overcome my fears and inadequacies', of self-doubt, low self esteem, and no self-worth. It seems like the words on those pages would leap off the pages and into my spirit, and energize me to put those words into action. I read books and learned of these great people: J. A. Rogers (The 100 Amazing Fact About the Negro) Carter G. Woodson (Mis-Education of the Negro) Ralph Ellison (Invisible man) James Baldwin (The Fire Next Time) Marcus Garvey the Founder of Universal Negro Improvement Association and African Community League (UNIA) Nat Turner (1831 Slave Rebellion in Southampton, Virginia) Denmark Vesey (failed revolt 1822) Madam C.J. Walker (1867-1919) Dred Scott (1799-1858), and many others.

My mind thirsts for more and more knowledge of my people. The floodgates of my mind were open, and my desire for reading was released. I felt that I owed my ancestors enough respect to be all that I can be, because it was their broad and courageous shoulders that I am privileged to be standing on today. The point here is, by me studying and learning that black people had done many great things contrary to what the images of (the tell- a- lie- vision), and the school system would have me to believe. I knew differently, so I began to feel good about myself, and when a person starts to believe that they are worth something and not worthless. They will receive power. That was the purpose of slavery to dehumanize the person, and keep them ignorant. The master knew had they had self -worth the power that they would possess, and that very power is feared today. If not tell me why do they; who is they? You know who they are? Why are black people always fighting for the same human rights as other human beings? It was and still is Black men and Black women, who are leading the movements of freedom that are benefitting all Americans.

I am determine to dispelled those negative beliefs that I thought were true about black people; that we were not as good as others people. See when a person sees, hears, and feel that they are worthless; they bring that belief system into reality, and that is exactly what I did. In the words of my younger counter parts, I flip the script on the lies that were embedded in my spirit. The message I want to convey is that a person can have a purpose driven life, and get from under that cloud of self-hate, self-doubt, and self- destruction. They must gain the knowledge of self, and that will equip them with the wealth to finance for better self.

I have had the experience, and the pleasure to know men who have made that self discovery and are now great men of character, so if I may, I would like to dispute the negative devices that are deployed to deceive the public that black men are uncaring savages like the movie Birth of Nation depicted. There are plethora of good black men out there who are nurturing, cultivating, loving, and are raising their children. Those images are not televised in the twenty- four hour news cycle. I want this book to inform people that black lives matter and that black people must be the narrators of their own stories. We have to replace their negative images and replace them with more positive images, because we have more positive things going on in our community. They are not televised in the White-Jewish owned media outlets.

Here is a list of a few men that I know personally who our contributing to their family and setting examples of what men of characters are to their community and throughout the world:

(1). **My good friend and a true man of morals and character Jahaad Abdul Shakur said, "In short I raised my children with the sense of African Royalty "overstanding" privileges and entitlement with that, and operating from a spiritual base it has been a successful recipe to witness them become productive members of society. I credit my Mother and Father who instilled in me morals, values, and principles. Brother Shakur is an entrepreneur who runs his own successful business, and has been happily married for over twenty three years. To support his business go to Children at Play on instagram Costumes/G@childrenatplay**

(2) **Tro; a young man that I had an opportunity to mentor who recently just passed his bar examine, and is expecting his first child. "I think fathers build connections with their children by taking part in their daily activities. Whether it's playing pitch and catch or helping them fill out college applications, these moments verifies to the child that dad will be there no matter the circumstance. When the father isn't there for these moments it creates a void in the child's well –being, and this void usually stays with them even as adults.**

(3) **Ken: He is a childhood friend who saw me go through my transformation from a boy to a man here is his perspective: First of all by being a father to my kids I try to teach them that education is the key to life, and how easy it is to go to the penitentiary. No matter how old they are so they don't make the mistakes I made. That it is never too late to go back to school because my friend Arnold is a good**

example of that. I stay in my kid's life because as a father it's my job. It is my job to teach and to motivate them to try to live successful lives, and to help others become successful. I just know it is important to stay in our kids lives. Thank you, Kenny Wayne for your valued perspective.

(4) **Anonymous perspective:** A women can raise a man to be what she wants him to be but a man can raise a young boy the way you suppose to, by instilling in him with the knowledge and wisdom that is required on his journey to becoming a man. Women and men are two different genders, and we have two different roles so by default genetically they are just certain things a woman cannot teach a boy as a man.

(5) **Minister Thompson perspective:** I am a firm believer that having a father in the home is vital in raising children. Even though my father was not around, my grandfather graciously accepted the role as our father figure and ensured my brother and I knew what it looked like to be the head of the household. He instilled in us to be God-fearing men dedicated to our families. He displayed qualities that I would not have experienced had he not been in my life to include but not limit to: How to respect myself first and foremost, how to respect the lady in my life, how to be a provider (he also instilled in us that the man should pay all the bills if possible), and how to be a father to my children and a father figure to all children. I thank God for having this glowing experience of having a father figure in my household. Therefore, I am adamant it is of the utmost importance for fathers to be in the home. I like to thank you Minister Thompson for being a true friend, and for being a man that other men want to emulate.

(5) **The Author's Perspective:** I believe to be a responsible father one must have pride and moral character, and those same moral characteristics will transfer over to their children. We also must realize that a woman through her valiant efforts, and her natural nurturing ways are not sufficient enough. There is a role for a male and their role is essential in raising a boy into a man. I like to use the analogy that a seasoned father told me, "that a woman is like a bird, and a bird just

cannot teach a lion how to roar." Therefore, a woman just cannot teach certain qualities to a boy. Men we must assume our responsibility and we must fight for the lives our children, because our children are being disrespected, and there is a certain entity that wants to kill and murder our children under the protection of America's laws. I say to the real men we must take up this battle to save our children from the evil powers that are working feverishly to reverse the hands of time. Our children are being slaughtered through the legal systems, education system, child support system, welfare system, health system and any other system that are not conducive to the welfare of our children. I say men put on your full armor and let's fight for the future of our babies. Men if we don't do it? Who will save our babies? I say Black lives matter, what do you say men?

(6)Mr. Hare's perspective: This is my friend who we started the ELITE YOUTH GROUP, one day just talking and next thing we knew it was a reality. Hare said, "In today's world a good father is a special thing. Youth today is in need of a fatherly love. We should be tending to the Garden of Eve, but we are dodging pit bulls in a jungle. Every real man is a father. He is ordained by God if he listens to what God says. He is a community, church father, school father, and etc. we must bring back the ability to communicate with our kids.

(7) My cousin Ramon L Chef: My cousin is an excellent chef who is also a conscience brother. My cousin said, "In my opinion Fathers are important for girls to know what a good guy looks like, and for boys to know how men are, but too often that does not occur due to the male ego a lot of us tend to fall short, but that's another story. We mean well, and we somehow work it all out.

(8) My good friend Clarence who I love like a brother. He is a retired Army Veteran who served his country honorably, and now he is serving his family and community honorably. He is leading by example what men of character are supposed to be, and I am proud to know him. Here is Clarence perspective on the subject matter: I feel it is extremely important for a child to have a father, in today's society with all the negative influences that we face as adults. It is double for a child, a

father, and not a dad. It is important to instill positive influences within their child, especially for our young black men. After all the bible says teach a child in the way they should go for when they get older they will not stray.

(9) **Cory a License Professional Counselor (LPC), who is working on his PHD. He is another example of a positive young man who negates the false perception of black men. Here is this young man's perspective: For males, it's simple. Fathers suppose to teach their sons how to be a man. Not a woman. Fathers teach your daughters how they should be treated by a man and learn how men operate.**

When I began writing this book, I was going to only insert the opinions of men and their views. However, things changed and the woman view is essential in raising and trying to understand this crisis that the American families are facing. The evanescing of fathers in the homes must be eradicated, by first realizing that there is a problem and begin a discussion with an open mind. Why this problem is allowed to exist and view it from an objective and subjective perspective. Here are the women views of why it is important for the male presence in the home and in their children lives.

(1). **Terri's perspective:** It all starts with your parents. When a child doesn't have a positive male figure in their life, they already feel the void of not being wanted and not good enough, why didn't he love me enough to stay are the questions we ask ourselves. Was I not pretty/good looking enough, was I not smart enough, was I not worth the love? All I wanted was the walks in the park, 10 minutes of reading, helping with my homework, kisses, time, but most of all LOVE. I guess that was too much to ask for. Having a father in your life builds your self-esteem, helps you cope emotionally, set standards for what type of man to look for. Parents they need to put pride and differences aside and love our children the way they should be loved. Co-parenting or staying with the parent may not work out, and it isn't easy but when you look into that child's eyes next time you see them, remind yourself that I won't let the curse go on any longer. I want my child to succeed and not what I we think is best for us. Or worst of all! We don't think we need a man because "mommy didn't need daddy." Or as little boy, he don't want to be a man, and when he someday have a child he thinks he doesn't have to be in there either. It's a GENERATIONAL CURSE that needs to be broken in most homes or there will never be peace. If we as women don't have a great example of a man, how in the world do we know what to look for? I guess we just go off intuition and be the change. There's only so much mothers can teach their young ones, and there are things that only daddy can teach them. Our kids should be our priority, and we have to do better. Give that child a chance at life and he will be there for you until death! That was the writer's daughter perspective. Her perspective was thought provoking and riveting. This touched my heart, and makes me more determine to create that bond and be there for her emotionally, and be a better father. Thank you baby and daddy loves you a million times plus infinity. By time this book is in print you will be in Chef School, I hope you pursue your dream of becoming a chef. I know you can do it because you're my child and we don't quit. When obstacles get in our way we go through them, around them, over them; but we don't quit.

(2) **The Honorable Judge Mays**: It is important that a father be involved with their daughters; this is her first interaction with a male. Fathers can teach daughter how they should be treated and how they should respond to different behaviors. My father told me that I was a Queen and that if a man could not respect you and treat me like my dad treated me then I don't want him. Also that love should not hurt, therefore let no man hit you because you already have been raised. Thank you my friend, and one of my many inspirations.

(3) **My brilliant friend Zee**: She goes far above and beyond what is required of her position as a case manager. Here's what she had to say: It's important for fathers to be a part of their children lives to influence the type of individuals they will become. With boys the father actions show them how to treat women and their kids once he is an adult for girls it shows them what to or not to accept from men when she's an adult. This is displayed off of how the father treats the mother of his kids as well as his kids whether the mother and father are together or not. Also men should be a part of their kid's lives because good fathers provide security

protection, prevent aggression, and give children more psychological and emotional stability than kids growing up in a single parent home with just the mother. I like to thank my friend and co-worker. Who I have confidence that she will succeed in her pursuit of excellence.

(4) I wonderful and brilliant teacher who has transformed the lives of many young black boys, and have replaced despair with self-knowledge which is a dangerous thing in a positive way. **Here is an article she wrote:**

WHY BLACK GIRLS NEED THEIR FATHERS

By: Jacquelyn D. Golden

I believe girls need their fathers or positive father figures to help shape their adulthood choices when it comes to men. A positive influence is critical to a girl understanding the definition of a good man. If her only definition of a good man comes from television, the streets, or rap music, she has failed before she can even internalize her own definition. She has too many other definitions infused in her head already. It becomes difficult to play catch up on what's real, and what's not. 72% of black babies, 53% Hispanics, and 66% Native Americans are born to unwed mothers according to government stats in 2008. This number has slightly increased since then. Because of this, they have already come in the word with a challenge. No "Father!" women can give all they have to a baby, but they can't give what a man can give. If two people are together the baby has a more whole and well-rounded personality.

History states and shows that African Americans were ripped from their homes of Africa, and brought here to be brainwashed, dispersed, degraded, mentally massacred, and physically tortured. Their mental state of mind was set up for following and failure, instead of leading and success. If a man is not used to being head of his house hold, provider, bread winner, and disciplinary; then is forced to become head of "NOTHING," he is thrown in a mental state of self-survival and not family survival. If a man never figures out who he truly is (a King), He will forever be lost in another man's kingdom.

Because daughters were snatched from their fathers in the very "beginning," society is having a hard time playing catch-up. Woman and girls alike starve for the male's attention because it has been absent in their youth and their life. Women often end up in abusive, neglectful, and misleading relationships because they marry their father's image (whether the father is there or not). Due to a lack of role models on multiple levels, this could be an alcoholic, a physical or sexual abuser, or someone with a mental illness.

When girls have positive images for a father, they are more capable of choosing a man that is caring, loving, employed, and supportive. Good fathers communicate to their daughters about what a good man (healthy inside and out) is supposed to do for her, and how he is supposed to treat her. If we want our woman and girls to make healthier choices themselves, we must first help who God made first, "THE BLACK MAN!"

WOW. POWERFUL!

Here are the views of our fatherless children who have been abandoned by the breakdown of America's moral decline: Q: how did it feel to not have your father in the home?

A: My name is Marquis growing up without a father figure can only do one thing, put hurt in your life but it's up to you to teach yourself how to be a man you are suppose to be. There will be plenty ups and downs and in the end you will be proud of yourself, because you did it all by yourself. Q: How did it make you feel emotionally?

A: I am frustrated, fed up, angry very aggressive and I don't trust nobody.

Thank you Marquis who I called my son, I saw a lot of me in him, and I really tried to work with him when I was there in South Carolina. I enrolled him in the youth program called Empower Leaders Innovatively through Education (ELITE).

I hope this book will began a dialogue for Men and Women of all sectors of society, but I chose to focus on African American, because that was my targeted audience. However, I am aware that white single unwed women are having babies born out of wedlock too, and their numbers are alarming as well. I want to take the blinders off of injustices not for African Americans, but for all Americans who are being subjected to things that they have no idea about. I still believe that love can conquer hate, and by talking about our struggles, pains, needs, and wants. Maybe we can make the world a better place for our children. My motto is, "uplift, not tear down your fellow brother or sister of God's Holy Tree." Because in the end when it all is said and done, all any of us have is the moment we share now. Make your now count! I need some warriors who are ready to stand up and resonate their voices into action. I need the brightest and the hardest workers to come up with more than just a march to feel like you're doing something. We need a strategic plan, and after the march an unrelenting effort by the masses to fight this war on genocide. We need a plan of action to fight the disparities' in these manufactured X factors of: juridical system, educational system, and the prison to the pipe line system. What is so humiliating everyone is trying to get so deep and come up with this new plan to the same problem? As I stated before, the formula to curtail the enemy is to know our history. The same methods that were used to get voting rights and human rights are waiting to be utilized; then they must organize.

What are the Solutions my People to these problems?

1. **How can we the people change the new laws that are suppressing the freedom to vote?**
2. **How can we amend a legal system that allows judges to ignore evidence and facts when the accused are black?**
3. **How can we restore the men who are put in jail for non-violent crimes drug acts, and when released from the modern day slavery plantations are stripped of their citizenship? They are not allowed to vote or carry fire arm to protect their property and families. They are left to be protected by a fraternity of men who view them as hostile. What about their second right amendment rights?**
4. **How can we stop the prison pipeline system that targets are preschool children?**

5. How do we gain respect from the political parties?

6. How do we reconnect and teach our people to be proud of who they are, and they don't have to feel inferior or act like they are beneath anyone, because they are original creators of knowledge and are the original chosen people and that is why the oppressor wants to destroy them. I want them to say it loud, that they are black and they are proud, and that they have a rich history. Let them know that they have made major contribution to the world. Had it not been for the labor and many of the inventions made by Blacks the world would have not made the advancements, and be in the position they are in now.

7. How can we convince poor rural whites, working poor, and the working class that we are in the same boat? Meaning that if you are economically disadvantaged because of low wages or you are part of the working poor then skin color doesn't matter. The 1% doesn't care if you are black, white or candy stripe. They don't care about you either. The only color they are concerned with is the color green (money).

8. How can we improve our greatest wealth, which is our health? How can we take the money and the big banks and profit out the health business so it can be more affordable for all, and not just for the elite to obtain outstanding health care?

9. How can we hold them accountable if they are not performing their job? How can we fire them if they are not meeting their performance requirements? They should be able to be fired just like the rest of us working citizens.

10. Where are the doers of the word? It is time to make a change and we are the people got to do it.

Thank you all and please contact the Solution Committee and provide your solutions and views. Proceeds from this book will go to the Elite Youth Program for the sustaining and building our future leaders. For speaking engagement contact the Solution Committee: 614-902-8629/803-387-3612

You tube/ Arnold Shurn
Facebook/ Arnold Shurn
Ashurnas@Yahoo.com

Printed in the United States
By Bookmasters